The Moves We Make

(Artists and Athletes book 2)

By CD Rachels

The Moves We Make

Cover Illustration Copyright © Story Styling Cover Designs
Professional beta read by Catherine at Les Court Services. www.lescourtauthorservices.com
Copy Editing by Karen Meeus. www.karenmeeusediting.com

(Synopsis)

Landon

On my university soccer team, people see me as an obnoxious loud-mouth, but this semester, I'm turning over a new leaf. Part of that involves supporting my best friend and his new relationship (with a guy!). Ravi being gay has really thrown me for a loop. The way he looks at Steven, it makes me feel... jealous? I'm not gay, but no girl has ever made me feel the way those two feel about each other. To top it off, I'm forced to take my university arts requirement in the form of a dance class! I have to fumble around trying not to fail while the teaching assistant Dane refuses to take it easy on me.

Still, the longer I spend in dance class, the more I get to know the real Dane: he's fun, interesting, sweet, attractive, and...did I say attractive?! No way, that's not what I meant. Because if I actually feel that way then... turning over a new leaf just got a LOT more complicated.

Dane

Dance is my life, and being a performing artist is my ultimate goal. That's why I took this university TA position and why I'm hoping to secure an internship in the big city. I refuse to get distracted by some admittedly handsome jock that I'm tasked with teaching. He's uncoordinated, but eventually, I can tell that he's actually trying, so I cut him some slack. There's also the tiny detail that he admits he may not be 100% straight.

That's fine by me. It's not like a guy like that would go for someone with a messed up face like mine. Still, as the weeks go by, something shifts and we become closer. I can't let myself become sidetracked in catching feelings for a boy who's new to being queer. I just need to disregard the burning chemistry we have whenever we're in the dance studio alone. It'll be easy to ignore the way he makes my heart flutter when he talks to me, or how charming he is when he lets down his guard.

Well...maybe one kiss won't hurt, right?

["The Moves We Make" is a low-angst, male/male romance, opposites-attract story involving hands-on movement lessons, road trips, drunken dance floors, soccer games, and discovering what love and sex with the RIGHT person can actually lead to, HEA guaranteed.

It is the second of the "Artists and Athletes" series but can be read as a standalone.]

* * *

To J. Thanks for playing video games while I trapped myself in the editing cave.

1: Landon

I'll admit that I can be a loud-mouthed idiot at times. I have a tendency to say things without thinking, including words that might be considered offensive, specifically homophobic slurs. Truth is, I've never had any problems with the queer community; I knew gay people existed, but I always assumed they were flamboyant types who wanted nothing to do with the things I liked—sports, video games, etc. While I never had any ill intent, I'd say derogatory slurs—think the *"F-word,"* insulting gay people—around the locker room sometimes. All of this was because of my upbringing and not personally knowing any queer people. I play on the Korham University division 2 soccer team and spend all my time with my teammates. When would I ever meet an actual gay person? Well this past semester, all of that changed. One of my best friends Omar Odom shared that he is bisexual; it's "not a big deal" according to him. Another close friend Ravi Metta came out as gay with a boyfriend of his own.

I was possibly the last person to realize my best friend had a boyfriend. Again, and I can't stress this enough, I'm a bit of a dumbass.

I'm sitting here at our end-of-semester Athletics Formal, dressed to the nines, and I look up to see him and his boyfriend, Steven, slow dancing. It's still jarring to me—two dudes romantically involved. Still, I see the look that Ravi gives Steven, and I know they're crazy about each other. Real love between two men…You don't see that every day! Anxiously, I watch them dance, hoping no one makes a scene. Instead, another close friend of mine Kareem Hall gets up with his girlfriend and proceeds to slow dance as well. Pretty soon, dozens of couples, college athletes with their dates, are all standing up, swaying to the music.

I turn to my date Tara. She's really hot—tiny waist, perky tits, full lips—really everything I like. Yet, I don't think about her the way Ravi talks about Steven; he's over the moon for his boyfriend, and I'm just lukewarm for this hot chick. "Do you, maybe, wanna dance?" I ask, even though that is the last thing I want to do. I'm only asking because it seems like the appropriate thing to do, and it dawns on me I do that a lot— say things because I feel like I'm supposed to, not because I want to.

"Not really, I'm not much of a dance person," Tara replies. She's looking down at her phone and I sigh a breath of relief.

"Oh good, me neither." I wait a moment, looking around, trying to come up with anything to say. Even though she is incredibly good-looking, I don't have any real desire to talk to Tara or hang out with her. "Um, are you liking the formal?"

"Oh yeah, my girls are so jealous I get to be here with a big soccer star like yourself." She says the words, but she's still looking down, texting.

"Some of my friends and I are gonna get some food after this. You wanna come?"

"We could." She finally looks up and throws me a mischievous stare. "Or we can skip all this small talk shit, and you can take me back to your place." She puts her hand on my knee, and I immediately get semi-hard.

"Sounds like a plan." I'm grinning now. She may be boring, but I can't let the night go to waste now, can I?

An hour later, we're both sweaty in my bed. I lie back, all orgasmed out, wiping my brow. As my breathing steadies, I turn over to cuddle only to see Tara getting up. By the time I realize what's going on and sit up, she's nearly dressed.

"Um, hey?"

"What's up?" She's fully clothed now, putting on her shoes.

"Did you wanna...hang out?" I get up, snap the condom off, and toss it in the trash.

"Oh, no thanks. I have a final in a few days, so I should go study."

"Oh," I reply, not bothering to hide my disappointment. Part of me wanted her to stay, but a bigger part is relieved I don't have to try to make small talk with her anymore. "Do you want me to walk you home?"

"Aw, Landon, you're sweet, but no thanks. This was fun. I'll see you around next semester, probably." She gives me a short wave and walks out of my room into my suite. A moment later, I hear the suite door close.

I sit back on my bed, dazed, trying to recall the events of

the night: Tara was hot. I got laid. I've been trying to get with her for like two months. Why do I feel disappointed?

Thirty minutes later, I'm walking out of the suite shower in just a towel when I see Ravi and Steven walk through the common area. They're still in their formal wear, laughing and holding each other; they don't notice me. Ravi unlocks his door while Steven kisses his neck from behind, muttering something about how hot he is. They finally make it in and I thank the heavens we each have private rooms.

I don't want to hear their sex noises, so I'm definitely not jealous of Kareem for having to share a wall with them. I'm also not attracted to dudes, especially not my best friend Ravi. So then why does seeing them happy make me feel so jealous?

Oh yeah, it's because tonight's hook-up was supposed to be something like that. I thought I would find a deep connection, the beginning of a serious relationship for the first time in my life. Instead, I got okay sex with someone who, frankly, I don't even enjoy talking to.

Ravi and Steven laugh and spend all their time together, and they're so clearly over the moon for each other. So yeah, I'm jealous. Why can't I have what they have?

2: Dane

We stumble into his apartment, and the lights are still off. I don't want to ruin the mood, so I intend to keep the room as dark as possible. We're both slightly buzzed from beer, but I want to chase this high. I'm horny, he's pretty hot, and it has been too long since I've gotten any sort of action.

Once I finally get him naked on the couch, I moan into his body, trailing my mouth downward along his abdomen. He's hairy, more bulky than lean, but I find him very sexy. As I take off my shirt, I refuse to reflect on the fact that I don't really care what he looks like. I just need to suck a man off tonight, and he's ready and willing. Finally, I get my mouth on his dick and get to business.

After five minutes or so of sucking him, he grunts—music to my ears—and I swallow him down. Now I'm feeling buzzed and satisfied. I'm palming my erection and wiping my mouth with my left arm when he suddenly turns on the lights and looks down at me. His face immediately drops in horror.

"What?"

"Your fucking eye is punctured!"

"What, no it's not!" I reply, annoyed.

"Did I break your eye?"

"No," I repeat, starting to get furious. "It's…always like that." I pick up my shirt and put it back on. That pretty much killed my boner.

"Oh," he replies, slowly realizing. Zack or Zeke, I don't recall his name from when I met him at the bar an hour ago, proceeds to put his clothes on. "Oh sorry about that."

"Don't worry about it." I refuse to look at him as I get up and make my way out.

"Hey, did you need me to…"

"No thanks. Um, I should get going."

"Okay. Thanks for tonight. I had…fun."

As I look up at him, his face is still filled with concern. He keeps staring at my bad eye. Fuck, I hate seeing that. It almost makes me regret not wearing the eye patch. "Same…I'm gonna go call a cab. See ya." I dash out of there before he can try to make any more small talk.

I sit on a bench outside as the cold January air bites my neck. I see my breath under a streetlight and shiver a bit, but I don't even care. Moments like tonight have become so commonplace that they barely piss me off anymore. I stopped believing I could get off or have relations with a man and be seen as a normal person a long time ago.

When I get back to campus, I go to the late-night dining hall to get something to eat. As I peruse the limited hot foods, I notice they're all out of chicken fingers and tater tots. I'm still a little buzzed, and I was really craving fried carbs, so I'm somehow even more disappointed now than I was thirty minutes ago.

As I exit the dining area, I see all the tables filled with my least favorite type of student, popular jocks. They teased and annoyed me throughout high school, but now here at Korham University, they just ignore me. This is mostly fine —I have no delusions believing any of those muscular guys would ever want to hook up with me, let alone date me. However, tonight I'm extra irritated just being near them. They're so loud, obnoxious, and eating all the food I wanted. Seeing their trophies all over campus annoys the hell out of me, and having to see them is just icing on the cake of a terrible night.

I finally make my way out of the dining hall and trek back to my dorm. At least I won't have to see any of those jocks after I graduate next spring.

It's Monday afternoon and I'm preparing to get to class. I check myself in the mirror before I head out. My doctor says I should wear the medical eye patch so that light doesn't bother my left eye, and also so that people don't notice how asymmetrical my face is. My left eye socket droops down and is purple like a bruise, but I don't even notice it anymore. Instead, I brush my short-trimmed brown hair and try to focus on my other assets.

My jaw is decent, right? I've got nice, full side burns and a good amount of stubble. As a performing arts dance major, I've kept in shape all these years, so maybe people will notice my abs before they notice my eye? *"Yeah, right. Keep dreaming, Dane-y boy,"* a nasty voice in my head chimes in.

I take a deep breath and decide to forgo the eye patch. I head out and make my way across campus to the Korham University Fine Arts building. It's my first day as a teaching assistant in Professor Ryn's "Group Dance Explorations 111" class, and I'm honestly so stoked. I finally get to impart the wisdom and knowledge in the art of dance I've gained ever since I was a preteen. Now, the important thing is I need to be assigned people who are talented, like my friend Val. I'm in charge of my choreography, and it will be part of my video résumé after I graduate. I want to make it as a performing artist, preferably in New York City, and I need good dancers this semester to really make myself shine.

I make my way through the basement corridors of the Fine Arts building. There are three small dance rooms, one of which will likely be mine to helm all semester—score! The rooms are all connected down a long dark hallway, with one large dance room at the end near the professor's office. Today I'm walking down to the large room to get my TA assignment for the semester.

Walking in, I see many familiar faces, mostly girls from dance classes I've taken here at KU for the past three years. I don't even bother to stop to chat as I dash across the room to the roster taped to the far wall. As I anxiously read my assigned group, I memorize each name. There are girls I know, but there's one name I don't recognize.

Puzzled, I walk over to the main dance faculty, Professor Ryn, who's sitting in a desk chair working on her laptop.

"Uh, hey Professor Ryn, I noticed the names you assigned me?"

"Hey Dane," she says, cheery as ever, but not looking up. "What's up?"

"There's one name I don't recognize. L. Landon?"

"Oh yeah, he's new. To the dance world anyway. He's on the soccer team or something."

"What?" I ask, in shock. Some soccer newbie?

"You know the Korham U Fine Arts requirement, and the

athletics department pleaded to get this guy in. Apparently he's one of the star players on the team or something."

"Yes, but can he even dance?"

"I don't know his experience level." She shrugs and casually turns off her laptop to go to start class.

"Is he even here yet?" I'm looking around in a panic, but there's no soccer guy in sight, only girls.

"Doesn't look like it."

"So he's late, meaning he definitely doesn't care about dance. Great!"

"Dane, I'm sure you can teach him a thing or two," she says, sounding frustrated. I'm whining, but I don't really care. "I'm starting class now." Everyone else begins to gather around her, and I stand there, wrapped up in my own thoughts.

Jocks already get everything at this school, and now we're making accommodations for them in the dance department. Just my luck, I'm TA-ing my dream class and now I'm stuck with some soccer guy who's going to slow me down. My semester is off to a fantastic start.

3: Landon

This year I'm turning over a new leaf. No more being obnoxious. It's time to discover the "new and improved" Landon.

I walk through the doors of the Fine Arts building and quickly find a staircase that leads downward. Today is my first day of "Group Dance Explorations 111," and while I'm not thrilled about having to take the class, I know better than to be late on purpose. Last spring, my academic advisor told me I didn't need to take an arts class, but apparently I wasn't listening to the final part of that sentence where she said, "in the fall." Everyone at Korham University needs to take an arts class, and with my soccer schedule, the only intro-level class I could take that seemed remotely tolerable was "GDE-111."

I gave Ravi so much crap for taking a drawing class last fall, so I guess this is karmic justice. The extent of my dance experience is grinding up on girls at the occasional club — even then I barely moved, so this promises to be embarrassing. Hopefully my two left feet will allow me to stumble through passing this class. Otherwise it'll be a pain in the fall to take an arts class and graduate on time.

"There won't be any grades at all if I can't find the damn classroom," I mutter to myself as I wander down the basement corridors. I know I'm running late, but the Fine Arts building is basically a maze. How can anyone find the dance rooms?

Eventually, I come upon a large hallway with the room numbers getting smaller. I pass by an empty room with a large mirror wall and smooth wooden floors—that looks dance-y to me! I keep walking and pass by two other identical rooms and hear sounds coming from the end of the hallway. Finally, I arrive at a larger room with lights on and people inside.

I burst through the doors, breathing heavily from all the nervous power-walking I just did, only to be met by the gazes of about eleven students —mostly girls— and one older woman, all wearing black leggings. You know, I may have had this exact fantasy in high school, but now that it's actually happening, I'm pretty embarrassed.

"Hi!" The older woman in the front, Professor Ryn I assume, beckons me forward. "If you're here for Group Dance Explorations 111, gather around." She turns back to the front before I can reply because apparently I interrupted her lecture. *Way to go Landon. You're on fire today.* "So Wednesdays we do basics together as a class, but today we're going to break out into the assigned groups early so you can get to know your TAs."

As Professor Ryn continues talking, I look around the room and try to collect my thoughts and my breathing. Some of these girls are gorgeous, with nice long legs in their black tights, but I feel completely out of place here. I know I'm in shape—soccer players have to be— but these chicks all stand with such poise...like at any point they're going to break out into a flash mob fit for a parade. To make matters worse, I'm wearing jeans! Why did I not wear my sweats?

I glance to my left and spot a rare sight- it's the one other guy in the class. He's also wearing the requisite black tights, and I can't help but notice how toned his body is as well. I try to smile at him, but he turns and looks away, a serious expression on his face. Hmm. I wonder if he's gay, like Ravi and Steven. Wait, why do I care?

Fifteen minutes later, the professor dismisses us to break out into our small groups where we will spend the majority of our time this semester. A bunch of people walk over to the far wall to read off their names on the group assignments lists. I finally find my name underneath the words "*Group A: Room B03: TA: Dana Poorweisz.*"

I shrug and walk out of the room to get to the nearby room B03. Whoever this Dana chick is, I hope she's hot. No wait, I'm not going to be shallow anymore this semester. My only hope is she'll go easy on me, considering my complete lack of dance experience.

I casually walk in and see the one other dude in our class standing by the mirror. He's stretching those long, muscular legs, the same legs I can't seem to keep my eyes off. I'm not really sure why his trim, tight body seems...interesting to me. Huh.

Okay Landon, new leaf, time to make friends.

"Hey bro." He doesn't acknowledge me. "You were forced to take this class too, huh?"

"No," he replies curtly, still not looking at me. *Stupid*

Landon. Why did I ask that? Of course dudes can want to take this class! So stupid.

After a moment I ask, "So...do you know who this Dana chick is?"

"Pardon?" he grunts at me, still not bothering to turn to his right.

"Dana is our TA. Unless I read the group assignment wrong?" I try to offer a smile.

"Are you L. Landon?"

"Yeah. And you?" I put out my hand for him to shake it.

Instead, he turns his head and roughly says, "I'm that *'Dana chick.'* You can call me Dane, your TA for the semester."

My face turns beet red as he walks past me. So much for that new leaf. I guess this semester I'm still going to be the dumbass who regrets half the things he says.

4: Dane

"Alright, so let's do some floor stretches while we introduce ourselves," I announce.

I get down and spread my legs, and the girls follow suit. This Landon guy takes forever to follow us, probably because the dumbass is wearing jeans to a dance class.

"My name is Dane. I'll be your TA this semester, and I'm really glad to be able to share the gift of dance with you all, as well as the audience." I lean over to my left with my right arm arching over my head to reach for my left big toe. "I hope to explore different styles of dance together as a group. Hence the name of the class." At this, the girls smile while Landon struggles to sit upright and move his arms.

The girls then introduce themselves. We have Val, one of my friends, and Tisha, a good friend of hers, whom I've taken some dance classes with as well. They both talk about how excited they are to be part of my group, all while the three of us stretch with ease.

Next, I turn to Landon who is finally able to touch his toe. I nod at him expectantly.

"Oh hey." He waves at the girls. "I'm Landon. I'm really new at all of this. Um, but I'm ready to...dance my ass off?" He chuckles like it's a joke, but my face doesn't change. I hope it's clear I'm not amused.

"Your first name is Landon?" I ask.

"Everyone calls me that," he replies, looking me in the eye. He's got a boyish grin and dirty blond hair. His face is symmetrical, and even through his shirt, I can tell his arms are toned. If his existence didn't annoy me, I'd probably be taken aback by how traditionally handsome he is.

"Okay, well, let's do some basics on the barre." I stand up to shake my mind of any thoughts of Landon being good-looking.

Val, Tisha, and I walk up to the barre that's attached to the large mirrored wall. We're holding it with our left hands, and we're turned to our right. Eventually, Landon follows suit. "First position," I announce. The girls and I immediately get into the ballet first position, with our heels in and feet turned out. I notice three people behind me that Landon is staring blankly at our feet, not moving, but I try not to let it distract me.

"Second position." We move our feet apart. "Third." We bring our right heels in to touch the middle of our left foot. "Fourth." We all lift our right hands and move our right feet forward. "And fifth." We bring our feet back in.

Of course, the entire time I'm announcing this, Landon's eyes bug out like he's a fish out of water. When I announce we're shifting to the other side, we all rotate so we're holding on with our right hands and facing the other direction. This leads me to the unfortunate circumstance of watching Landon in the front, failing at each position I announce. I sigh internally. This is going to be a disastrous semester.

As we walk out of the studio at the end of class, I want to catch up with Val, but Landon jogs up to me first.

"Hey Dana."

"It's Dane."

"Right." He winces. "Dane. Um, I just wanted to say, that was a really good class."

I look around and see no one else, so I nod at him, skeptically. He takes that as his cue to continue. "You uh, know a lot about ballet."

"I've been taking dance classes since I was eleven," I reply, curtly.

"Right. So you could tell I was kind of lost?"

"One of my eyes works." I shrug.

"Ah…" He scratches his head, looking down. I try to ignore the bulge of his triceps. "Well maybe you can slow down during our next session?" He looks up at me with a pleading look in his eyes. Oh hell no.

"Look, we've got a lot to get through this semester." I start walking backward. "Maybe you should consider dropping this class if you're not cut out for it."

"What?" he exclaims, trying to keep up with me as I walk into the hallway. "No, no way. My coach already pulled massive strings to get me into this class. And…and if I drop it, it'll mess up my season this fall, and soccer is really important then, and—"

"Well this class is important to me!" We both stop, and my face is mere inches away from his. "This is my major. I refuse to let some guy who's never danced before mess up my TA position because the athletics department dubbed him so special he could join in. You're not exceptional!"

A flash of hurt crosses his face and I realize I'm being a bit harsh. "Bro...Screw you, you don't know me." He pauses to close his eyes like he needs to collect his thoughts. "You need to chill. I am trying to be a better—"

"We'll see how well you *try* during our next session, Landon." Once I'm done, I dash up the stairs. It isn't until I get out of the building that it dawns on me that maybe I went too far.

5: Dane

Three days later, I'm in one of the upstairs rooms of the student union building, putting down stacks of plastic cups. This large space is the dedicated headquarters of the "Queer Pride Union," the campus group dedicated to all things LGBTQ. We hold weekly meetings, have fundraising events, and even have office hours as a safe space for anyone questioning themselves. This week is our "Welcome Back Mixer," and as a member of the executive board, I have to help set up.

"Dane, people are already showing up," Dominic says. He's the president of the executive board, a big teddy bear of a dude with a deep voice, and a good friend of Val's and myself. "Do you wanna crank the music, or should I?"

"Go for it, boss." I smile as he plugs in his phone and the bass starts booming to a Britney Spears track. I move on to the next table and start lining up the pamphlets and complimentary safe sex paraphernalia— condoms, lube packets, etc.— as Dominic goes to open the door and let folks in.

---

* * *

Thirty minutes later, the room is crowded, and everyone seems to be having a good time. We have people playing video games, board games, and plenty of folks chatting and having drinks—non-alcoholic, because this is a campus event. I'm talking to Val at the front of the room when Dominic turns off the music.

"Attention everyone!" Everyone turns to him and a quietness takes over the room. "Thank you all so much for coming to the 'QPU Welcome Back Mixer.' On behalf of the E-board, I, Dominic, just want to announce some happenings for the semester. First of all, we want to welcome our newest faculty advisor, Professor Wong." He points to the lean man standing next to him.

Everyone applauds while Professor Wong waves at everyone. "Please, call me Wei. I'm happy to be working here at KU and even happier to help out with Queer Pride Union. Although, this is Dominic's show along with the rest of the E-board. I'm definitely not in charge of any of this." He shakes his head, and we all have a laugh. Wei can't be more than ten years older than us. He looks like he could still be twenty-one.

"Well, we thank you for being here," Dominic says. "I want to announce again that we'll have our regular meetings on Tuesdays starting next week, along with 'Safe Space office hours.' Wei and I, as well as the rest of the E-board, will be rotating to provide confidential help to anyone who shows up. If you or anyone you know is questioning themselves or needs guidance with identity issues, please reach out or come visit us during office hours."

"Or just come to hang out. It gets lonely sometimes!" I shout. Everyone laughs as Dominic nods.

"We're looking forward to an awesome semester. That's all for the boring stuff. Enjoy, hang out, and let's get back to me playing some Nicki Minaj songs." The room applauds while Dominic turns the music back on.

With speeches over, I walk over to grab a bag of chips and I see two familiar faces by the snack table. "Steven, Ravi, you made it!"

"Oh hey Dane." Steven greets me with giving me a half-hug, like most guys do. "I didn't recognize you without the eye patch."

"Can't be in pirate costume every day." I move to give Ravi a half-hug too. I met them both at Val and Dominic's Halloween party last semester. I told them both to come to QPU meetings, and now that Ravi is officially out, I guess they can both attend.

"How's the semester going?" Steven asks.

"It's chill. I'm on E-board again, and I'm happy to be taking advanced dance classes."

"You don't happen to be in a class with a blond soccer guy, do you?" Ravi asks. Oh crap.

"Landon?" I cringe as he nods. Of course they're friends, Ravi is the co-captain of the freaking team. "Yeah, he's in my class."

"Why the face?" Steven giggles.

"He's not...um..."

"Let me guess. He's a loud-mouth who's already pissing you off?" Ravi grins at me. "It's okay. He's my best friend, but I know he rubs people the wrong way."

"It's not that," I reply, putting my hands up. "He's uh... trying..."

"But he sucks," Ravi says, bluntly.

"I might have bitched him out for not being good enough." I cringe.

"Harsh bro," Steven comments.

"I'll admit it was pretty messed up."

"Look he's a good guy deep down, I swear. He's not trying to be a fuck-up."

"Especially after last semester," Steven mutters, looking off to the side.

"Babe, that's in the past," Ravi says lovingly, putting his arm around Steven's waist. Steven blushes and looks him in the eyes.

"You guys are gross." I chuckle. "Okay, okay, I'll try to go easy on him the next time I teach him."

"You're *teaching* him?" Ravi stares at me in disbelief.

"Yeah. I'm the TA for our dance class. Why?" At this, Ravi and Steven give each other a knowing look. "What? What is it?"

They both chuckle and cuddle closer. Ravi puts both arms around Steven's waist and places his head on his boyfriend's shoulder. "All I'm gonna say is, I hope he learns to love the arts as much as I did." At this, Steven grins and kisses Ravi behind him.

"You guys are weird." I grab a bag of chips and walk away, shaking my head. I don't know what they were implying. Nothing is going to happen between me and a straight soccer jock who doesn't know a thing about dance.

6: Landon

I'll admit I screwed up last week, but today I'm determined to turn over that new leaf, starting with getting to class early. I'm even wearing black sweatpants and everything, ready to make group dance my bitch—note to self, *"Don't say that out loud because it makes you sound insensitive."* As I walk toward the large room where we all convene on Mondays, I can't help but overhear Professor Ryn down the hall. I don't mean to eavesdrop, but when I hear the second voice, I can't help myself.

"And your group is doing fine?"

"Yeah." I recognize the distinct voice as Dane's. "We get along well."

"I knew you would with Tisha and Val. You've worked with them in the past. But how's Mr. Landon doing?"

"He's doing fine," Dane replies. That's the second lie he's told in ten seconds, and both of them are about me!

"Are you sure? I know you had your reservations. If he's not making a true effort, I can urge him to drop the class."

"No need, professor. With the strength of his soccer legs,

he'll pick up the choreography in no time at all, I'm sure of it. I think he has potential. He's already proven he can keep up, and I'd like to develop the four of us as a group."

"Well alright then," Professor Ryn replies. "In others news, did you send in the audition video?"

"Yeah, I did, right before the semester started. Hopefully I'll get the callback…"

They discuss some dance audition Dane is going on while I creep away. What the hell was Dane talking about?

Class today is more of the same. I fumble the beginner ballet positions, while the girls try to ignore me. This time, however, I'm in my sweats, so I'm able to move my legs more freely. Also, unless I'm mistaken, Dane is going over the moves more slowly, maybe for my benefit?

Throughout class, I watch everyone else's feet in order to learn the moves. I notice that Tisha and Val have nice glutes and thighs, but I find myself staring mostly at Dane in his black leggings. As a soccer player, I've seen guys naked in peak physical condition, but Dane's body is different; he's toned, but he carries himself with the poise of a performing artist. When he stands still at the barre it's…fascinating. I don't know why.

"*Nothing gay about that*," my inner voice notes, sarcastically. *Shut up, inner voice.*

After class is over, I manage to get Dane alone again as we leave the room.

"Hey man, thanks for going slower in class today."

"Don't mention it." He's refusing to look me in the eye. Now that we're not at each other's throats, I take a good look at him. He has nice cheekbones and stubble I wish I could grow. He has a drooping eye, but who cares about that with a jawline like his? He'd probably be attractive to me if I swung that way. *"What do you mean 'if'?"* my inner voice asks.

I try to push away all my bi-curious thoughts and focus. "Look, I just want to let you know…I heard you speaking to Professor Ryn before class."

He awkwardly looks left and right. "Eavesdropping is kinda rude, Landon." He's chastising me, but it's not as harsh this time.

"I happened to be standing there, and I heard my name."

"Well, you shouldn't have heard that." He tries to walk away, but I keep up.

"You totally vouched for me. Why'd you lie?"

"Who said I was lying?"

"You said I have potential in dance!"

He finally stops and turns to look me in the eye. "Maybe you do."

"Seriously?"

"Landon, I kind of…judged you harshly last week. That wasn't fair. As someone who's gotten prejudged his whole life because of this"—he points at his left eye—"it doesn't make sense for me to do the same to you."

I'm touched by his seemingly sudden change of heart. I also have the urge to defend him from people who would make fun of him for his eye. "Oh…well, thanks."

"Again, don't mention it." He full-on grins now. "But just so you know, we'll be doing jazz and Latin choreography next week. I won't be slowing down, so we'll really see if you have dance potential or not. Anyway, peace!" He dashes away and I'm left standing there stunned.

My chances of being dropped from this class by the

asshole TA? Minimal now. My chances of falling flat on my ass in embarrassment? Higher than before, somehow.

7: Landon

Saturday mornings are for brunch with the boys. It's not that I eat, sleep, and breathe soccer—though in the fall semester, I kind of do—but it's more that I spend all my time with my suitemates. I'm fortunate enough to room with my best friends who are also my teammates, and on weekend mornings we like to get up early to get the best breakfast a college student can afford at the dining hall.

I somehow manage to snag a table for the four of us, but as I see the other guys approach with their food, I realize four chairs are not enough. Kareem walks over with his girlfriend Stacia and they sit across from me while Omar sits next to me, wrapped in a hoodie, most likely working off a hangover.

While Kareem grabs a chair for Stacia, Ravi sits down diagonally from me, and Steven is with him, pulling in another chair. This small table barely has any space with the six of us jutting around it, but I'm still feeling like it's a good morning with my boys.

"So, what party or bar should we hit up tonight?" I ask excitedly.

"Please don't talk about alcohol right now," Omar

The Moves We Make

murmurs before sipping his hot coffee.

"I can't, I'm having dinner and a movie with Stacia's family tonight." Kareem smiles at his girlfriend and they gaze at each other fondly.

"Okay..." I reply, trying to hide my disappointment while poking my eggs with a fork. "Ravi?"

I look over to see Ravi spoon feeding some oatmeal to Steven. The two of them look like they're going to pounce on each other right here in public. "Uh, Ravi?"

"Huh?" he asks, finally turning to me.

"What are we doing tonight?"

"Oh, Steven and I are busy." They turn and grin at each other.

"Great, now I gotta hear *that* through my bedroom wall tonight," Kareem replies, smirking and shaking his head.

"I think they're adorable," Stacia remarks.

"Guys, the spring season is right around the corner. We need to take advantage of our free time while we can."

"I think that's exactly what *they're* doing," Omar quips, pointing at Ravi and Steven, who have leaned in and whose noses are now touching. "Anyway, how's dance class treating you?"

"Good. Learning a lot."

"You gonna be a prima ballerina soon?"

"Oh definitely." I grin back at Omar. "I'm going to be a regular *Fred Astaire-Michael Jackson* hybrid. Just you wait until the semester show."

"When is it?" I turn to see Steven asking, and now the entire table is looking at me.

"What?"

"When is your semester show?"

"Uh..."

"We're definitely going," Omar says.

"Yeah, we wanna support you," Ravi adds, his voice laced with sincerity.

I nod. I had no idea they actually wanted to see me dance. Now I'm really afraid of looking like an idiot.

"I'll...let you guys know." I slink back down in my chair and sip my orange juice.

The rest of brunch goes by uneventfully as the couples in front of me shower each other with affection while Omar tries not to fall asleep to my right. I watch Steven make Ravi smile brighter than I've ever seen, and just like the night of the Athletics Formal, a weird sensation flashes through my chest.

I definitely don't have feelings for Ravi, Steven, or any other guy. Still, the connection I thought I felt with Tara wasn't actually there. I want someone who makes me laugh and smile, who takes care of me. I want someone who sees me on my worst days and still thinks I'm worth it. I don't wanna hook up with random girls— I want someone to be my solid ground.

Maybe I haven't met the right girl yet, but if someone as close to me as Ravi found happiness with a guy, it's possible I can find that kind of happiness with a dude as well. Hell, Omar hooks up with guys and girls and seems to enjoy that life. *Two* of my best friends in the world are queer.

I'm looking for someone who will make me feel content, and I'm willing to look beyond the bounds of my up-until-now exclusively heterosexual existence.

Twenty minutes later, I'm throwing away my trash in the bin underneath a large bulletin board. Campus events are regularly posted here, even some parties, so it's worth checking out from time-to-time. One flyer catches my eye: it reads, *"Questioning who you're attracted to?"* among other inquiries, and has a bright rainbow border around it. Underneath, it details the "Queer Pride Union Safe Space Office Hours," which takes place on campus. Shit, maybe they can help! Before anyone notices, I snap a pic of the flyer on my phone and walk back to my dorm.

Yeah, I have questions, and hopefully I can get answers.

The following Monday, I'm walking up the steps of the student union building to get to the QPU room, and my hands won't stop shaking. My whole world has revolved around chasing after girls, and now I'm going to question that by talking with some random person about my sexuality? I know they are supposed to keep it confidential, but that doesn't make it any easier.

I review the facts in my head.

Number one, I used to think gay guys didn't lead the kind of life I did, but Ravi disproved that.

Number two, girls are hot and all, but no girl has ever made me feel a real connection, like the love Ravi and Steven seem to share.

Therefore, number three, my next logical conclusion is to consider dating or hooking up with guys. Unlike in the past, I'm finally thinking things through before I jump into them headfirst. Hopefully 'Safe Space' will help answer my questions.

As I muster up the courage to enter the QPU room, I see a slim Asian guy behind the desk fiddling on his phone. He looks up and smiles, his eyes lighting up the room. "Hey! Are you here for office hours?"

"Uh...yeah," I reply, my voice trembling. I sit down across from him.

"My session ends in about six minutes, but I'm more than happy to talk to you until then! I'm new to KU so..."

"Oh, cool?" I'm starting to sweat. Is it hot in here?

"Look at me, babbling on and on. Let me start over." He looks up and shakes his shoulders a bit. He's kind of adorable and handsome, in a professor sort of way. "I'm Wei. I'm the faculty advisor and for this hour I'm running QPU Safe Space office hours. Anything you say here will be held confidential, unless you're planning on hurting anyone."

"Got it."

"So how can I help you?"

"Well...I'm not sure."

I look down and twiddle my thumbs. *Am I really going to say this out loud?*

After two whole minutes of silence, Wei finally says, "You know, I came to terms with my sexual orientation when I was about your age."

"You look like you're still my age." I chuckle nervously, deflecting.

"Good genes." He shrugs and smiles. "Anyway, there are certain conversations you need to have with yourself, but we at Queer Pride Union are here to help talk you through things."

"Gotcha." I really want to start talking, but the words refuse to come out—much like me.

After another two minutes of silence, I see Wei look at his phone. "Shoot," Wei curses, immediately getting up.

"What?"

"I'm sorry, but my ride is here." He proceeds to pack his

bag and I start to stand up. "Oh, don't get up. The next office hour is run by another member of QPU. He should be here any minute now to relieve me." I nod and sit back down.

"We'll talk later!" Wei dashes away, and I hear him in the hall, saying "Hey, there's a student already in there, so go do your thing."

I look back down at my trembling hands while I wait for this mystery person to show up. Am I ever going to be able to talk about this? When I see who's running the next office hour, I realize the answer is probably a no.

Seated in front of me is Dane.

8: Dane

"I have to say this before we start...My name is Dane, I'm the vice president of Queer Pride Union, and I'm running this office hour of QPU Safe Space. Anything you say here will be held confidential, unless you're planning on hurting anyone."

I put my hands together on the desk and try to remain neutral sitting across from Landon. Of all the people I could think of, he was literally the last person I expected to see at QPU.

"Dude, I know who you are." He's making it sound like a joke, but he actually sounds nervous.

"I'm mandated to say that for every student."

"Wei gave me the same speech."

"Then he's a good man." There's an awkward pause as we silently look around, avoiding each other's gaze. "What did you want to talk about?"

"Uh..." He looks down at his thumbs.

"You're not here as like a prank, right?"

"No!" he replies indignantly.

"Alright!" I raise my hands. "I believe you. I promise. So,

what did you want to talk about?"

"Um…" He scratches the back of his head and I once again catch a glimpse of his sexy arm muscle. *Focus, Dane.* Landon is obviously serious and nervous about being here. I took an oath when I joined the QPU E-board to run Safe Space office hours in an accepting manner. I need to support him in any way I can.

Another moment of silence passes, and it's clear he's too nervous to say what's on his mind—which is totally understandable when you're questioning your sexual identity. After more awkward quiet, an idea strikes me. "Do you play video games?"

Landon looks at me puzzled. I get up to turn on the nearby TV and Wii console. "Do you want to play Smash Bros on the Wii?"

A smile slowly breaks out on Landon's face. "Do you have GameCube controllers?"

I smile back. "Landon, this isn't amateur hour, of course we do." He laughs, and I immediately hand him a controller and bring a chair close to him so we're both seated equidistant to the TV. As the game fires up, I notice we're less than a foot apart. My dick takes an interest in the idea of me sitting closer—preferably on his lap— but I quickly squash that hormonal fantasy.

Landon is just a jock who can barely dance. We have very little in common. So what if he's questioning his sexuality and he's kind of attractive? It doesn't change the fact that nothing is going to happen between us.

"Your ass is mine, Poorweisz." My eyebrows jump as I glance at him and see him grinning at the TV. I really wish he hadn't said those exact words.

* * *

We spend the next several minutes laughing and trash-talking as we play the fighting game. Four Smash Bros matches later—we each won twice— Landon leans back and looks down, his face turning serious again. I feel tension build between us, but I don't want to interrupt this moment.

"When did you... How did you know you were..."

"Gay?"

"Yeah," he replies, his voice barely a whisper. I hear him swallow, and he's still not looking at me.

"I guess...it was around puberty. The other guys talked about boobs and long hair, and I realized my ideal partner was someone more masculine...with a toned body."

"Huh." He's still not looking up.

I take that as my cue to continue. "When I think of someone I want to date, someone who really makes me happy, I picture someone with a deeper voice, a toned, athletic body, and shorter hair. That's really all it boils down to." I look up and see him staring at me already. Did I say too much?

"Gotcha. Well...I guess I'll see you in class on Wednesday." He's looking at me intently, but I don't know why.

"Definitely."

He stands up and puts his fist out and I bump it. He smiles and darts out the door. Landon is the one who came here for answers, so why am I the one with more questions than before?

The next two weeks go by in a flash. I get a couple of visitors at 'Safe Space' office hours, but when no one's around, I catch up on homework. Each week I feel a small sliver of hope that Landon will show up to talk more, but he doesn't. I want him to visit for his sake, but also, a small part of me enjoyed hanging out with him, just kicking back and playing video games. It's a little selfish, and I'm not trying to get him in bed —though I wouldn't be opposed to that—but I don't have that many close guy friends here at KU. Hanging out with Landon outside of class felt really fun, and I feel even worse about being an ass to him on day one.

Speaking of which, in GDE-111, things are coming along as well as can be expected. After each class, I wait for Landon to bring up his visit to QPU, but he makes no mention of it; I promised confidentiality, so I say nothing.

His dancing is, well, as uncoordinated as ever. He's improving little by little, but I need to switch up the styles every week. I think he enjoyed my intro to Latin choreography, but otherwise he's still struggling to keep up. Despite this, I know he's working hard, and I can't ask for too much more. I cut him extra slack, knowing he's possibly questioning his sexuality, but I pray he improves soon so I can start putting together our group showcase.

Speaking of showcases, today I walk into class on my phone, and as I see the subject of my latest email, my heart starts to race.

"Val... Val..." I say, tapping my friend's shoulder, not bothering to look up.

"What's up?"

"I just got an email from the Regal Dance Company of Manhattan."

"Shut up!" Her eyes widen in shock. "The RDC Manhattan?"

"Yes!" I squeal, not caring that Tisha and Landon are standing nearby. "You know how I submitted my audition video?"

"And they replied?!" She's gripping my hand now.

"It says here, *'We are proud to offer you a callback interview for the position of Performance Intern'*!"

"Holy shit, congratulations!"

"Thank you!" We're both screaming and hugging now.

"Congratulations, Dane," Tisha says, walking closer.

"Yeah, congrats man," Landon adds. "You're gonna ace that whatever it is."

"It's a big deal!" I exclaim.

"I believe you." Landon looks at me, smiling.

"When and where? What are the details?" Val asks.

I look at my phone. Shit. "It says it's in Manhattan this Saturday. Fuck." My stomach drops. There's no way my parents are going to be able to drive me there.

"What's wrong?" Val asks.

"I don't know if I can make it on such short notice. I don't have a car. I mean, maybe I'll take a bus?" My shoulders slump in defeat. The biggest opportunity for a dancer in New York, and I might miss it?

"What street is it on?" Landon asks. I look up at him, puzzled.

"Uhh, 86th...Upper East Side. Why?"

"I can probably drive you. My house is not too far from there. Talk to me after class." He smiles and shrugs, a hopeful gleam in his eye. Walking backward, he says, "We should probably get started if I'm ever going to master *tombé-pas de bourré.*"

"Hey, you remembered what they're called!" Tisha replies, gives him a high-five, and they both laugh.

I got a callback from my dream internship, and Landon is gonna get me there? And he remembers the name of a dance move? This is too much information for me to process right now. I shake my head and get to the barre to start leading stretches.

After class, I find myself fiddling with the bottom of my sweater while I wait for Val and Tisha to leave. I bite my lip as Landon approaches me, an easy smile on his lips.

"So...were you serious about...You know..."

"Friday night? Going to Manhattan?"

"Yeah. Um, my aunt lives in Queens, so I can probably go stay with her."

"Dude, Queens is far. Just stay with me and my family. That way you'll have plenty of time to get ready for your audition!"

I can't argue with that, but his generosity is killing me. "I don't want to impose."

"I'm offering." He smiles again, like it's not a big deal. Dammit, stop making me like you.

"Um..."

"How about you chip in for gas? Then you won't owe me anything. Plus, you'll be keeping me awake on this car ride. That's kind of like contributing!"

"I suppose that's true. This audition is a huge deal," I mutter to myself and mull it over in my head, looking down.

"I'm going down there anyway, Dane." He shrugs and takes out his phone. "If you're down, you let me know. Plug in your contact and I'll text you where my car is."

I hesitate, then take his phone. Landon's favor feels like a massive debt, but I need to get to Manhattan. "Okay. I'm down." I nod and plug in my contact. "Thank you, Landon."

"Well alright, see you then." He smiles a dazzling grin and walks out. I stand there dumbfounded. If I was uncomfortable with Landon being some random jock in my class, he and I becoming friends somehow feels scarier.

9: Landon

It's Thursday evening and I'm in the locker room, happy to be done with practice. I love being on the field, but these winter practices are chilly, so the warmth of the showers is much appreciated. The spring semester games barely count toward anything, but Coach Dacks doesn't want us to get complacent.

As I'm putting on my shirt, I notice Kareem giving me a concerned glance.

"What?" I ask.

"Are you alright man?"

"Yeah, I'm fine."

"You let a freshman steal from you today during scrimmage and you didn't moan about it."

"I hadn't noticed." He stares at me while I pull out my phone. "I gotta make a call."

I walk out of the locker room and hit dial. A moment later I hear my mom's voice. "Hi sweetie."

"Hi Mom. I just got out of practice."

"I didn't think you were playing in the winter."

"Nope. I'm still playing." My family really doesn't notice what I do in college. They've never noticed anything I've ever done that I was even remotely proud of.

"Well, I got your text. You needed to talk?"

"Yeah, it's about this weekend."

"Oh your brothers and sister are so happy you're gonna make it this year!"

"Right." I nod, biting my lip. Last year at this time I made up some excuse as to why I couldn't come home this specific weekend. "I wondered if I could bring along a friend of mine? He needs to come to Manhattan on short notice and I offered to drive him. He probably won't even be around for the party."

"Of course, sweetie, you know the house has plenty of rooms."

"Thanks Mom." We chat a little bit longer about my classes before I bid her goodbye and hang up. When I walk back into the locker room, I notice the guys are filing out.

"You good man?" Ravi asks, picking up his bag.

"Yeah, just had to remind my Mom I'm going back home this weekend."

"Oh nice, have fun!"

"Thanks." I gather the rest of my things and catch up to him. "What are you up to now?"

"I'm having dinner at the union with Steven and a bunch of people. Wanna come?"

"Ah, no thanks, I've eaten too much union food this week. I'm just going go study or something." This is a lie, but how do I tell my best friend that being a perpetual third wheel isn't fun?

"Alright, later!" Ravi says, not noticing my obvious discomfort. He smiles as he looks at his phone, no doubt texting Steven.

That Friday once classes are done, I haul my bag down to the campus parking lot. I texted Dane to meet me there, and lo and behold, I catch him sitting on a bench. He's holding a large duffel bag and seems nervous; I'm not used to seeing him like that.

"Hey."

"Hey!" My car unlocks with a honk nearby, and we both walk toward it. "You all set to go? Need to use the bathroom?"

"I'm good." He's nodding and looking at the ground while I open the trunk. The energy between us is awkward, and I really don't know why.

"Is the air okay? Need the windows down? Or the heater up?"

"No, it's all good," Dane replies enthusiastically. We're on the highway off campus now, headed south to New York City. "Thanks again. I really appreciate the ride."

"No problem." I look at him and he smiles at me uncomfortably. "Though I guess I should tell you my ulterior motive."

"What?"

I chuckle at him. "Relax, it's nothing major. The reason I'm going home this weekend is because my family is having this big gathering that they do every year in the winter. See, my brother and sister are twins, and it's their birthday tomorrow, and my older brother has his birthday the day after."

"Okay," Dane says. "That sounds nice."

"Except they rope me into it even though my birthday's not for another week."

"Ah, I bet sharing a birthday sucks."

"It does, but it's more boring than anything. My parents invite their friends and small talk with them the entire time. All they do is go on and on about how amazing my siblings are, but if I bring you along, I can say, *'Hey, my friend needs me,'* at any time and peace out."

"So I'm your excuse."

"Exactly!" I shoot him a grin and he smiles back.

"I didn't realize we were such good friends." He laughs uncomfortably.

"Hey, we played Smash Bros together. That makes us friendly!"

"Oh…I didn't know if you wanted to talk about that day." My eyebrows jump, and I look over to see a face filled with concern. "We don't have to!" Dane quickly adds. "Talk about it. Confidentiality. And all that shit."

I smile. "Not much to talk about. But I'd appreciate it if you didn't tell my family."

"Of course!"

"I don't want them thinking I'm gay."

"Right."

"They're cool with it though. They're super accepting of the LGBTQ community and all their employees who are gay, so you don't need to be worried."

"Glad to hear it."

"Besides, if they start shit, I'll defend you." I smirk. I look over to see him smiling at me already.

"Thanks. So, you've realized you're not gay." He sounds delicately neutral.

"No. With all the girls I've hooked up with, no way." I shrug. "But I've realized, I can't write off guys either."

"Ah."

"It's like, girls can kiss girls all they want, but the moment a straight guy wants to experiment, he's like branded for life and burned at the stake."

"I hear that. Blame the toxic patriarchy."

"Word." I nod in agreement. "But to settle your question, I'm not gay, but...I don't know what I am."

"Of course. You deserve to think things over for yourself." Those words pull at my heart strings. Dane seems to understand what I'm going through and isn't judging me. I assume that's part of a QPU position, but still, my respect for him grows. I look over at him—he looks so sincere, and I smile back. When he smiles, his bad eye also curls up, and I find it very cute.

"So you think Dane is cute now, huh?" my inner voice whispers. *Shut up inner voice.*

A tense silence grows between us in the car. Before I can turn on the radio, Dane says, "Uh... I'm going to look over my dance videos and try to think about the choreography, for the callback."

"Right!" I nod enthusiastically. "I'll leave you to it, friend." I give a faux salute for good measure.

That's how we spend the next three hours—Dane on his phone, and me concentrating on the road. I'm totally not focusing on the guy in my car, the same guy I'm getting closer and closer to every day.

10: Dane

I wake up early and get dressed in a room that isn't mine, and thoughts of last night resurface. Oh, that's right, I'm in Landon's guest bedroom.

He and I got dinner last night at a highway rest stop. We made small talk about our favorite foods and things to do in Manhattan. I thought it would be an uncomfortable meal, but it just felt like two people who have been friends for a while.

"I'll leave you to it, friend." Landon's words echoed in my mind. He may be straight-but-questioning or bi-curious or whatever complicated label works for him, but he's labeled me as one thing, a *'friend.'* I'm totally fine with that. It makes things less messy. He's opening up to me, and it sounds like he needs to do some experimentation. He's 100 percent not interested in doing so with me, though. Besides, he's kind of like my student, and there'd be ethical ramifications if I were to kiss him.

Not that he wants to kiss me. He probably thinks my face is fucked up, like everyone else. I'm fine with all of that.

Last night we arrived pretty late at his house in

Manhattan, with Landon parking in his family's designated garage spot. When we walked into the foyer, most of the lights were off and he led me straight upstairs. I didn't get a good look at any of the other rooms because we both immediately passed out—my guest room is the room next to his. I'm belatedly realizing just how rich Landon's family must be.

It's not enough that he's handsome and a popular jock. Of course he's wealthy too. *Focus, Dane, this guy just did you a massive favor. Stop being a bitter bitch.*

In daylight, I walk down the grand staircase with my bag over my shoulder, following the smell of coffee. Turning the corner, I see several people around a dining table, only one of whom I recognize. A blond guy and girl look up at me, and Landon's head turns around as well.

"Hey, good morning!" Landon says. He stands up to pull out a chair for me—how chivalrous! "Guys this is Dane, my…friend from school."

An older woman at the front looks up from her tablet and sips coffee before saying, "Hello dear! How'd you sleep?"

"I slept well, thank you, um…"

"It's Mrs. Landon. Honey, your eye looks all sore. Did you sleep on it?"

Landon's head whips around so fast. "Mom!" he whispers loudly. He's trying not to embarrass me. That's kind of sweet.

"It's okay. It's always like this. The bed was lovely. I can't thank you enough for letting me stay here." After all these years, I'm a master at deflecting questions about my eye.

"Ah," Mrs. Landon replies, trying to interpret what's going on. She stares at Landon and me perceptively. "Well, any friend of Landee's is welcome here."

"Hi!" the girl to Landon's left chirps. "I'm Kara, Landee's sister."

"And I'm Link, his brother. Nice to meet you." I'm taken aback by how gorgeous they both are. Kara is conventionally good-looking, and even seated, Link looks massively tall. It's very possible Landon is the least beautiful person in the family—by traditional standards. Am I feeling sorry for Landon? That's a shallow thought, so I push it away.

"Come join us for breakfast," Link suggests.

"Thanks, but I gotta run. I have a big day ahead of me. I just wanted to say hi."

"I'll walk you out!" Landon says, ushering me out of the kitchen area.

Once we make it to the foyer, he hands me a MetroCard. "Now you can take the subway."

"Thanks man." I look to my left and right awkwardly as I stand at the open doorway. "Um...why does your family call you Landee?"

It's almost comical how quickly his face turns red. "Wait, no way...L. Landon stands for Landee Landon?"

"Look, not even the guys on the soccer team know about this." He's still refusing to look me in the eye, and I'm trying not to laugh. "So I'd really appreciate your discretion."

"Okay...*Landee*."

"Ugh." He groans, but there's a hint of a smile on his face.

"Last time, I swear," I chuckle. Messing with him outside of class is fun. His blushing is adorable.

"Alright *Dana*," he says with a smirk. "Go to your callback."

"Right," I reply as he guides me out the door. "See you later."

"Break a leg! You're gonna rock this! You're the best dancer I know! I believe in you! TEAM DANE!" He hollers and waves invisible pom-poms and I chuckle and wave back. Huh, my very own cheerleader. As I open the gate to the sidewalk, I try to ignore the butterflies in my stomach. Those are just because of this big meeting I'm about to have; that has to be the only reason I feel this way.

When I get to the train station, I wait at the crowded platform. I turn to my left and see a little kid holding his mom's hand, and he's already staring at me. Kids are cute, so I smile at him.

"Your eye is all *broken!*"

My face falls into a frown as the kid gets pulled away by the mom. "Don't talk to strangers like that!" she says as they walk down the platform.

I sigh in frustration and dig into my bag to pull out my eye patch. *"This is just easier,"* I say in my head as I cover up my left eye.

"Dana Poorweisz?"

"That's me," I reply, with my head through the door.

"Come in, have a seat. We're ready for you." The woman at the desk motions for me to walk in.

I step into the small office and sit in the chair across from her. The Regal Dance Company of Manhattan headquarters is in a small but ornate theater with several dance rooms scattered throughout the building. I've been led by a security guard to a small room by the stage for my interview.

"We're so glad you could make it. I'm Evelyn Ramos, and these are my associates Yessa and Tucker." The woman points to the people seated to her left and right and I shake hands with all three of them.

"I'm Dane. Nice to meet you." I'm trying not to sound nervous, but this meeting could change the trajectory of my career as a performing artist—no pressure.

"Dane, we just wanted to say we were so impressed with your audition submission." Evelyn smiles at me, and Tucker and Yessa nod. "You seem to have a firm grasp on different styles of dance, and with this performance internship, we want to cultivate someone who's just starting out to potentially become a permanent member of our dance company."

"That all sounds amazing." I grin, and the three people in front of me smile back. "So, how does this callback work? I've prepared a couple of routines to show you. I can even do group work if you'd like, or partner work if there's anyone you want me to dance with, either Latin or ballroom—anything really!"

"Oh," Evelyn says, looking to her associates. "I'm sorry Dane, I thought we made it clear in the email: this meeting was more of a get-to-know-you session and to iron out any potential logistics. We don't need you to dance today."

"Oh!" I hope I don't sound too disappointed.

"We really were impressed with your work and we're aware you're a dance major in college?"

"At Korham University, yes."

"Then we're perfectly pleased to just talk about what the internship would entail. We apologize if that was unclear, or if you prepared any long routines for us." She chuckles. "You won't be dancing for us today, but we appreciate your spirit!"

"Oh it's fine," I reply, chuckling as well. "Whatever you need, I'm your man!"

"Great," Evelyn says. "So it's a ten-week paid internship,

but there's a possibility we may need you for several more months..." We spend the next thirty minutes talking about what the internship requires as well as my passion for dance. Afterward, I'm out of that building in no time.

When I get back to Landon's house, the party is well under way. Landon buzzes me in through the gate, and I notice he's changed into another outfit. He's got on a dark black suit, white shirt, and blue tie, all of which is fitted to accentuate his athletic body perfectly. I try not to drool as I greet him. *Focus, Dane. He's a straight-but-questioning jock, and you're just friends.*

"You're back so soon," Landon remarks while following me up the stairs to the bedrooms.

"Yeah, it turns out they didn't need me to dance. I wore these sweats for nothing!" We both laugh as I walk to my room.

"Well, I'm sure you impressed them anyway." We pause when we reach the guest bedroom and he stares at me. "What's with the eye patch?"

"Oh, this?" I forgot that I still had on my medical eye patch. "It's nothing."

"Do you need an eye patch? I've never seen you wear one in class." He sounds concerned but sincere.

"No, I don't need it, medically or anything, it's just...I put it on sometimes...like in public. It's just easier, less questions asked, and plus it makes me look..." My voice trails off and I look down, scratching my scalp. Why do I suddenly care what Landon thinks of me?

"Do you like using it?" I finally make eye contact again, and Landon seems stern but not judgmental.

"Um...It hides my bad eye from others, which is nice."

"That's not what I asked. Do you *like* it?"

I shrug, my face heating up. "Not really. Unless it's like Halloween. I feel like it singles me out."

"Then don't use it." I look up into his eyes. He seems so serious. "You shouldn't wear something that makes you uncomfortable. You look fine without it."

If this were four weeks ago, I'd think Landon was mocking me. Today though, I know he's being honest and genuinely concerned. Something warm fizzles in my gut and moves upward, and it's not the remnants of my lunch. I can tell he's being sweet and sincere. He's looking out for me. *What am I feeling?*

Landon clears his throat and looks to his left and right. "So you gonna come join us for dinner? The guests are all arriving."

"Um..." I shake my head to clear it of any funny thoughts and look down at my outfit. I feel so poor compared to the Landon family. "I didn't bring a suit."

He tilts his head and squints his eyes. "I bet I can loan you some of my clothes. Why don't you shower and I'll bring you some."

"You don't have to."

"Please, Dane." He looks me in the eye. "I want you to hang out with me at this party. Please? Pretty please?" Between the suit and Landon's kind eyes, how can I say no?

11: Landon

With Dane back early, I'm relieved to know I'll have someone to talk to this year at the family party. The twins will be too busy being pimped out by my parents, and my family doesn't want me to camp out in my room all day, so Dane being here is actually a life saver. I can only hope we can become better friends before my siblings reappear and do what they usual do—show Dane how un-special I am by comparison.

Going through my closet, I manage to find an old dark-brown suit and a white button-down I haven't used in ages. They're still clean, and I'm sure they'll fit Dane, so I grab them and some black dress shoes and walk next door to the guest bedroom. I lay out all the clothes on the bed and stare at them intently as if they'll soon reveal to me some secret code.

"Hey, you're back!" I hear Dane close the door behind me.

"Yeah, I got you some— " My words are cut off as my brain short-circuits. Dane is standing in front of me all wet and wearing only a towel. The remnants of shower water dribble down his rippling abs, and all of a sudden, I can't speak. I knew dancers were fit, but I didn't realize Dane was hiding the body of a Greek god under all those sweaters.

"Nice! A brown suit!" He thankfully doesn't seem to notice my thirst. "Thanks, Landon!"

He walks over to the bed and puts on his white boxer briefs right in front of me under the towel, then lets the towel drop to the floor. Now that I have a direct view of his sculpted ass packaged in thin fabric, I can say for sure he's *nothing* like the chicks I've been interested in before. Yet, with his back on full display as he pulls on my pants, it feels like... Do I think Dane is sexy? I can't stop staring at his body, and these urges are pulling me toward him just like during puberty when I started jerking off to girls, but...Dane isn't a girl. That would mean I'm...

I shake my head and take a step back. "Uh..." He turns to look at me. His right eye is so soft as he puts on the button-down shirt. "I'll meet you downstairs!" I bolt out of there and shut the door, trying to catch my breath.

I stand outside by the buffet table, putting dressing on my salad. The inner courtyard of our house has been set up with a dozen round tables and heat lamps because it's winter. Twenty guests roam around, most of whom are either chatting with my parents or talking to my siblings—Link, Kara, and my older brother Lars with his wife. Eventually, Dane makes it outside, and *fuck*, is he hotter with the suit on than he is half naked? Is that a thing?

I try to push down all these bi-curious thoughts. "Dane! Come get some food!" I smile and wave him over.

"Thanks man. This is"— he looks around— "lavish."

"My parents like to do it big for these parties." He smiles at this and starts putting food on his plate. Eventually we sit down at a table in the corner away from the crowds.

"You think you got the internship?"

"I hope so. They seemed genuinely interested in me."

"I hope you get it too. Just think, if you get it, since I live nearby, maybe we can hang out in the summer."

I eat some salad and look at him. An expression I don't recognize flashes across his face before he smiles again. "For sure."

We continue eating in a comfortable silence for a minute. "So why didn't you invite any of your soccer friends?" Dane asks while eating a piece of chicken parmesan.

"Honestly, I don't really want the guys to see me with my family. Life is…different here."

"Different how?" His face is etched with concern.

"I'm gonna need a beer if I wanna continue this conversation." I get up to grab some much needed liquid courage from a cooler.

When I return, I see my sister standing by our table chatting with Dane.

"That's amazing," she beams. "The RDC Manhattan!" I stride up to them and hand Dane a beer.

"You're a gentleman. Thank you," he says.

"Hey Kara." I look at her, dubiously.

"Landee, your friend here is so talented."

"Yup."

"I think that's wonderful." Thankfully, someone near my parents is waving her down and she waves back. "I gotta go mingle, but it was nice meeting you Dane. Hey, remember us when you're this big time choreographer!"

She and Dane chuckle as she walks away, and I take a long swig of beer.

"So you gonna tell me why home life is so weird for you,

Landee?"

"Well for one, I don't want the team to know my first name." He nearly spits up his beer, and we both laugh for a moment. "And number two..." I look around at all the people chatting with my parents and brothers and sister. "Isn't it obvious?"

Dane shrugs. "Your sister seems nice."

"She's way too perceptive, that one."

"What do you mean?"

"Look, me and my siblings, we're cool but...Kara, Linkara is her real name, she's a genius. She's graduating with three majors next year. And Link, he's like this six-foot-six tower on his university's basketball team. He does modeling sometimes." I sound so bitter, but I can't help it. I take another sip of beer. "And my older brother Lars is already running half of Dad's company and he has this gorgeous successful wife who's a doctor."

"Those are all good things."

"Yeah, I know, and I love them but...I don't know. I can't help but feel jealous."

"I can understand that. They took your birthday too."

"Exactly! All my parents' friends are so impressed with them, and any friends I brought home before would rather talk to them than me. I've even had girls over who started flirting with Link. And it's like...between the looks and the talent...Dane, you know I'm a dumbass. I can't compete with them in anything!"

"You're not a dumbass," he mutters. I swear I see him blush as he looks down at his food. It's pretty sweet to know he's defending me. A moment of silence passes between us while I eat a piece of chicken.

"I'm sure your friends will still like you, even if they meet your family."

"Thanks." I smile down at my plate and eat some more salad. "I'm just glad you haven't been seduced by the rest of the Landon family yet!"

"And you and I are friends now!"

"Exactly! I'd venture to say we're becoming good friends." We both laugh and clink our beer bottles.

We spend the next forty-five minutes eating and chatting about everything and nothing in particular. Maybe it's the alcohol talking, but I think we're getting along very well. Dane is interesting, funny, and he doesn't make fun of my stupid, family-based insecurities. I'm wondering how we would get along if we were at a restaurant, just the two of us, which sounds suspiciously like a date.

At some point, Link walks up to us holding a drink. "Hey, what are you guys up to?" He towers over us since we're sitting down and has to bend down just to hear us.

"We're just talking about a class I'm taking this semester," I say, looking up.

"What class?"

"It's a group dance class I'm the TA for," Dane replies.

"Oh, that's cool! You're a dancer and a TA!"

Here it comes…the moment when Dane starts to like everyone else in my family more than me.

"Yeah." Dane's eye flicks to me then back up to Link. "Your brother here is a pretty fast learner."

"Oh really?"

"Yeah, I'm sure he could join BTS soon if he wanted." We all laugh, and I playfully shove him.

"That's awesome. I bet you all look great on stage," Link remarks. Is he flirting with Dane? If he is, I might throw up. I've never actually thought about my brother dating anyone, guy or girl. I down my beer, and Dane once again flicks his eye to me.

"Thanks. Hey Landon, do you wanna go upstairs so I can show you that video of those dance techniques I promised?" I stare at him, perplexed. "It'll help for class."

"Right. Uh, sure. See you later, Link." We both get up and throw our plates away.

"It was nice meeting you. Hope your birthday was fun!" Dane says, patting Link on the shoulder as we walk away.

"Oh right, you guys have stuff to do…" For a moment, Link looks down, his face etched with an emotion I don't recognize, then he looks up with a smile and continues, "Well, it was nice meeting you too. Night!"

When we make it up the stairs to our respective rooms, I chuckle. "You're not really gonna show me dance techniques right now, right?"

"No, I was, um, getting chilly. And sleepy." He smiles and I know he's lying.

"You didn't have to make an excuse to get out of there on my account."

"It wasn't for you! Your brother was…totally boring." He smirks and I let out a small chuckle.

"Sure, that's definitely how people describe him." I roll my eyes and smile at him as I open my bedroom door. "But thanks. You made tonight…actually fun."

"What are friends for?"

"Right. Friends like us." I look down and pull a piece of lint off my shirt. "Well. Goodnight Dane."

"Night Landon." Right as he opens the door to step into his room, I hear him say, "Oh, and for the record, your family seems cool, but I think you're just as bright and talented as any of them." With that, he walks into the guest bedroom and shuts the door. I'm taken aback and my face feels hot as I walk into my room.

I unbutton my shirt and ruminate on everything Dane said tonight. I think about his lips, his jawline, his eyes, and his shirtless body. There's no denying my bi-curiosity now, but I didn't think Dane would be someone I'd feel so attracted to.

I lie on my bed in just my boxers and his words echo in my head, *"I think you're just as bright and talented as any of them."*

It's amazing how someone I've known for such a short period of time manages to take my breath away so frequently.

12: Dane

"This is a great responsibility. I'm trusting you," Landon proclaims, with an over-dramatic sternness.

"This is an old mp3 player," I retort, scrolling through the device.

We've been on the highway for thirty minutes and he's just now asking me to use his device to pick a song.

Last night, I had a hard time falling asleep in the comfortable king bed of the Landon family guest room. They had been gracious hosts, but my twenty-four hours with them had injected a whirlpool of thoughts inside my head, all centered around one guy. Landon wasn't the party boy jock I thought he was; he had so much baggage in his home life, yet he smiled so sincerely whenever he was with me. I liked discovering all these different sides to him. He was kind, generous, and seemed to legitimately care about my audition and my well-being. Plus, hanging out with him made me laugh and smile. I thoroughly enjoyed spending time with him. Hopefully when we got back to campus, we could continue to be friends.

"*Friends with benefits?*" my inner voice asks. Shut it.

* * *

I snap back to the reality of the car ride at the sound of Landon's voice. "Hey, those songs got me through high school. I listen to them before a game. And now I'm trusting you to make this trip back to school entertaining."

"Alright," I reply with an unimpressed grin. After a moment of scrolling, my eyes light up. "No way!"

"What?" After pressing a button, heavy beats start playing, and Landon starts to smile, a blush spreading over his face.

"'Where My Girls At' by 702?"

"Hey, I like throwbacks!" Landon retorts defensively.

"I love this song!" I'm hopping up and down in excitement.

"You do?"

"I like nearly anything I can dance to." I proceed to sing along while doing a small locking dance in the passenger seat of his car. I bend my wrist up and down to the rhythm while I nod along. After a few beats, I look over to see Landon grinning at me. "What?"

"Nothing," he chuckles, shaking his head. Is his face redder?

"Are you annoyed by my dancing?"

"No! You look good. It's just...the guys would totally judge me for having such a girly song."

"I stopped caring about what people think about me a long time ago. You should do the same, *Landee*." I poke him for emphasis while smiling, and he giggles. He said I look good. What does that mean?

"I'm trying to be genuine with the people around me this semester, turn over a new leaf, and be a better person. I need to self-improve." He's smiling, but his confession seems so serious. He keeps alluding to something that he wants to make amends for. Landon has all these layers to him, and a part of me wants to keep digging until I see the real him. Maybe I already have.

I feel like we're encroaching on something too personal for him, so I let it drop. Instead, I focus on the music and pick another song.

"Wow! 'Are You That Somebody' by Aaliyah ?!" I squeal with delight.

"I'm a 90's R&B fan." He shrugs as I change the song. His smile is charming, and he seems so relaxed as he nods his head to the beats. "I didn't think you'd care for this music."

"I told you, I like many types of dance, including hip-hop."

"You and I have a lot more in common than I thought."

"Well, we're friends now. You're just getting to know me." He looks at me, his eyes flaring with an emotion I refuse to interpret. I simply smile and look down, reminding myself that Landon and I are just friends.

The universe decides to play a cruel trick and shuffle the next song to be 'They Like it Slow' by H-Town, the most sexually charged song I know. We both glance at each other uncomfortably before returning our gaze to the front. "Um… I can change it if you want."

"I don't mind. I like this song." Landon clears his throat. He's fixated on the windshield; he's driving, of course. His face looks a bit redder still and is it hotter in here now? Should I roll down a window?

I can't help but get lost in the sensuality of the song. As the singer describes caressing his lover's body, my eye keeps flicking to my left. Landon is sitting right there, with his toned arms and masculine scent. My gaze traces a vein that goes from his wrist up to his sleeve. I stare at his neck, his perfect jawline, and finally down at his crotch. I wonder what his dick looks like, and my gaze shoots back up in an effort not to cross anymore creepy lines. *Stupid sexy song.* I thank the heavens we're on a highway, because if we were parked, I'd feel the urge to reach over and kiss him. Frankly, I still do.

After a long three minutes, the player shuffles to a faster pop hit and we go back to laughing and obnoxiously singing along. *"That moment was a fluke, a byproduct of that sexy song,"* I tell myself. It's not like Landon has any interest in me anyway, so I push those thoughts away for the rest of the car ride.

"Two, three, four, ONE. Two, three, four, ONE!" It's Monday, and I'm shouting out the beats in our small group dance session. After I complete my small routine with Tisha, I step back and watch Landon and Val pair up and do it.

As I shout the beats, I watch Val dip in Landon's arms, get pulled up, spin twice, then step back. As she does, Landon steps forward with his left foot and they both raise their right arms simultaneously, curling their left arms forward to the mirror. Val has it down pat, but of course Landon still needs some work.

"I know that look," Landon says, cringing at me in the mirror. "Was it that bad?"

"Your arms are good!" I try to sound as optimistic as possible. "But um..."

"My feet suck." Landon's shoulders slump in response.

"Why don't we take a five minute break?" I suggest.

"Good, I need to pee," Val says, picking up her bag.

"Me too," Tisha chimes in, and soon they're both gone. Landon walks over to the barre on the mirrored wall and stares intently at himself. He's shaking his hips, but he lets out a frustrated sigh as they move stiffly.

"Hey, Latin-style hip work is hard. Don't beat yourself up."

"It's just annoying. I wanna keep up with the three of you," he whines, still staring at the mirror. I frown and walk up to him. The poor guy is really struggling.

"Here, let me show you some things. Let's start with your posture." I stand behind him to the side and stare at my reflection. "Your upper body needs to be taller, even when you're spinning and dipping Val." Landon tries to stand straighter. "Chin down and shoulders should be…"

Moving directly behind him, I put my hand on his shoulders, and they slowly relax down. "Good. Now your upper back should…" I place my fingers on the top of his back below his neck, and he straightens his posture. His skin feels smooth and warm, and I'm reminded of how chiseled every part of him is. *Soccer players, what can you do?* "Okay," I continue. "And your hips need to…"

I look down. Landon's ass truly is a work of art, but I need to be professional. "Can I um…"

"Do what you need to do." His voice sounds rough like he's struggling to breathe. "You can…touch my hips." *Why is my throat dry all of a sudden?*

I reach down and place my hands on his hips from behind. "Try moving like this," I say quietly. I guide his left hip forward while moving his right hip back. I feel his ass flex a little as he complies with my motions.

Damn, that just made my dick perk up a little. *Stupid jocks and their sexy bodies. Focus, Dane.*

I move his right hip forward, then repeat the entire sequence two more times. For some reason, I'm holding my breath as I do this, and the silence in the room tells me he is too. Finally, I let go, and like a child riding a bicycle, Landon shakily starts to do the moves on his own.

"You got it," I breathe out, my voice barely a whisper. I look up to see him staring intently at me in the mirror. His eyes flick up and down at my reflection. I'm standing so close to his back, mere inches away from his neck. I watch him lick his lips, all without breaking eye contact with me through the mirror. *Fuck that's hot.* Blood leaves my head and flows downward, and my skin starts to buzz. I don't know what's happening, but we're both in this now. I want whatever this moment is. I need...more.

I carefully, gently, place my hand on his upper back again, but this time I leave it there. Landon closes his eyes, and I feel his heat. Once again, neither of us is breathing. Inch by inch, I slowly bring my hand down lower, tracing the length of his spine through the fabric. I feel every curvature between mountains of back muscle. As I caress his lower back, a moan just barely escapes his lips, and it sends even more blood straight into my cock. I start to tent my pants, my dick reaching out to the ass that's millimeters in front of me.

It's like I'm not myself, and I somehow feel compelled to keep going. My hand finally grazes the very top of his well-defined glutes. I shift my hand downward so now I'm cupping the entire cheek. Landon moans again, a bit louder, eyes still closed. As my fingers curl into him with more strength, he leans back. This causes his ass to graze against my semi-hard dick, and lightning courses through me, making me curse under my breath.

I instinctively wrap my left hand forward onto his hip. I want, no, *need* to grasp the obvious tent in his gray sweatpants. My hand gets closer to his crotch and—

"And I can't believe she said that!" Tisha says as she and

Val walk back into the room. I immediately bolt away from Landon, and he does the same, walking in the opposite direction. The girls are deep in conversation and don't seem to realize what they almost walked in on.

Frankly, I don't know either.

I discreetly adjust my cock in my sweats, knowing my hard-on is to blame. I was thinking with my penis, and that is *not* okay. Not here, not now, and especially not with *him*.

I announce that we're doing some more Latin technique for the rest of class—solo work, because I don't want to touch anyone right now—and it's back to business as usual. I push away all my horny thoughts and go back to focusing on the lesson. I don't know what's going on in Landon's head, but I need to get a grip.

13: Landon

"Good work everyone! See you next week for small groups again!" Professor Ryn shuts off the music, and the entire class disperses. It's now Wednesday, and I'm thankful I don't have to be in a confined room taking lessons directly from Dane. I basically ran out of there after class Monday, and I haven't spoken to him since.

The memory of Dane's hands on my hips—and back and butt—has been haunting my every waking thought. The feeling of him tracing my spine turned me on like nothing I'd ever felt before. When he grabbed my ass, I immediately got hard and needed more. He was so close to touching my cock before the girls interrupted us. The scariest part was that I totally would have let him!

Dane wanted me; those caresses weren't part of any damn dance lesson.

I've been weighing the pros and cons of trying to hook up with Dane. On the one hand, he's hot and we have a lot of fun together. Most importantly, he doesn't treat me like a dumbass, but instead, like I can actually be a better person. He's met my siblings, and he still chose me, and I just can't get over how solid that makes me feel for the first time in my life.

On the other hand, he's my TA, he might not even want to date, and he has better things to do than waste his time on the dumb jock who's just now dipping his toes into the waters of bisexuality. It's settled then. I just need to forget about this stupid crush. "*Fat chance,*" my inner voice remarks, the traitor.

Now, as class is breaking up, I spot Dane talking to Tisha and Val on the side, near the exit door. I guess I have to walk by and acknowledge them. I'll just say a simple greeting and be on my merry way. That way, Dane and I can put any weirdness behind us.

"Hey man." Dane greets me, and the girls look at me too.

Okay, just greet him like a normal acquaintance. "Hey, do you wanna go out this Saturday for my birthday?" The words fly out of my mouth before I can stop them. *What kind of bullshit was that?*

"What?" Dane asks, eyebrows raised.

"Do you...guys all wanna go out? For my birthday. Downtown. Maybe dancing. At the Mousetrap?" The Mousetrap is this dingy bar that everyone in our university goes to at one point or another. While Dane looks skeptical, this seems to pique Val's and Tisha's interest.

"They have that new dance floor area," Val comments, grinning at Tisha.

"My boyfriend and I have been looking for an excuse to go downtown," Tisha adds.

"Great! That's five of us! I'll drive."

"Um..." Dane looks at me, then the girls. Val gives him a strange look, and he finally turns back around. "I guess...

since it's your birthday. It could be fun!"

"Nice! Oh, and by the way, I won't be in on Monday. We have our first away game that day. My coach informed the professor."

"Oh," Dane replies, his face falling in disappointment. Fair enough.

"But hey, maybe I'll learn a thing or two on the dance floor on Saturday, eh?" Val and Tisha giggle, and I immediately exit the room, not waiting for Dane to have second thoughts.

Instead of trying to "friend-zone" Dane, I accidentally invited him out to a bar to dance with him. I can hear my inner voice deadpan the words *"Way to go, Landee."*

Saturday night I drive our little group downtown to the bar. By the time the five of us find a table, the dance floor at the Mousetrap is packed. At least, I think it is. It's so dark in some areas that I can barely see the people I came with. The DJ in the back makes the lights flicker to the rhythm of the music. The bass is booming and patrons are moving and swaying to the beats.

I'm sitting at a table with Dane to my right. Across from us, Val, Tisha, and Tisha's boyfriend, Jonathan, are all chatting. "We're gonna go get drinks!" Val announces, and the three of them leave before I can get a word in.

Despite the noise, I'm acutely aware of how alone Dane and I currently are. Hopefully he can't see me staring at him through his bad eye, but I can't help myself. He's wearing a nice striped button-down shirt and dark jeans— it's a sexy look. I lean in and he immediately turns his head.

"You having a good birthday?"

"Yeah." I smile and he nods. I feel the tension from Monday

returning. I don't know if I should tell him I like him or that we're better off just friends. "Hey, I uh…need to tell you something."

"What is it?" He stares at me expectantly.

"I uh…" *Out with it, Landon.* "I've come to the realization that I'm…I'm probably not…100 percent straight."

Dane looks at me for a moment, then smiles. "Well, alright. Congrats on realizing it. That takes a lot of courage and introspection. I hope you discover whatever it is you actually are."

I look directly into his eye and try to summon the courage to say more, but nothing happens. Even in the dark, he looks so gorgeous. Being near him makes butterflies flutter around my stomach, making me a nervous wreck. Screw the reasons why I shouldn't. I want to kiss him, I want to shoot my shot.

Just then, the others return with their drinks, and the moment is lost. I lean back while Val talks about some girl she saw at the bar. "I'm gonna get a drink," Dane says. Before he can leave, however, the bass immediately hits hard and changes to a new song. Dane's eyebrows jump, and Tisha and Val gasp with a smile.

"This is our song!" Val yells excitedly.

"We did a routine to this last semester!" Tisha squeals, hitting her boyfriend's shoulder. "You remember the choreography, right, Dane? Let's go!" They rush around him and he's grinning now, shaking his head, but he lets them drag him away.

Jonathan and I follow them to the dance floor area, and, by some unseen force, the crowd makes way for the three of them. With Dane in the middle, they break out into a full choreographed set.

I've seen Dane dance before, but never a full hip-hop

routine. The three of them hit every beat with precision, confidence, and flare, but I can't keep my eyes off Dane. He's magnetic, he's fantastic, and he commands the dance floor. The crowd hollers, cheers, and claps for the trio, but all I can hear is my own heartbeat speeding up with admiration and desire.

When Dane is dancing, he's in his element, and that element is sexy as fuck. His legs twirl him around, his arms move in intricate patterns, and he smiles with a self-assurance I've never even had. Fuck, if I wasn't queer before, I am now. Dane is beautiful, and I want him.

When the song is over, everyone cheers while the music shifts to something slower, with more guitar riffs. Tisha walks over and grabs Jonathan by the hand. "This song is 'Reggaeton' by CNCO and Little Mix, and it's my jam!" She announces this to the four of us as she drags Jonathan over to dance, and soon, Val is dragging me over too.

The vibe is lit and everyone is having such a good time. I can't help getting lost in the music myself. I sway my hips while holding Val's hand, and we both laugh. She sings along to the song, waving for Dane to dance closer to us.

A crowd has mingled with the five of us, and as I dance, I feel like I'm on fire, but in a good way. The music brings the moves to life, forcing my hips to shake to the rhythm; this must be how real dancers feel every time! I glance at Dane who's swaying along, eyes closed, with an easy smile on his face. Seeing him like this, the music compels me to move closer to him. The words to the song remind me how much I want to taste him.

I finally get close enough to put one hand on his shoulder. He opens his eyes but doesn't stop moving, and neither do I. I need to chase this moment, even in front of all these people. I look him square in the eye and put one hand on his hip. We sway to the beat, and now we're synchronized. My thighs connect with his, and our faces are only inches apart. My heart is pounding in my chest. I want him so badly, and he's not stopping me. There's no one else in the room. It's just me, Dane, and the dance floor. Gazing at him, I move even closer, aiming to put my lips on his.

At that moment, the track changes to a louder rap song, and I look up to see a few lights turning on and off. When I look back down, I see Dane with a concerned look on his face, and he pushes my hands off. Suffice it to say, the moment is ruined.

"I need some air," he says, pushing past Tisha and Val. I follow him.

We make it outside the Mousetrap and the winter air cools the sweat on my brow. I follow Dane as he power walks down the sidewalk around the corner. I start jogging to catch up to him and see he's standing against a wall. His eyes are closed and he's breathing heavily.

"Dane, are you alright?" He opens his eyes and looks at me. Before I can say anything, I feel him tug on my shirt collar. The next thing I know, my mouth is on his.

14: Dane

With the way Landon was looking at me in the darkness of the bar, I had to get out of there. I needed to remind myself of all the reasons I shouldn't pursue him. He's new to being queer, this is probably just an experiment or a game to him, I have to teach him in class—*so* many reasons. Still, the moment he started dancing closer to me, I faltered. Then, when he put his hand on my hip, it was game over for me. Thank God the song changed so I could clear my head.

That didn't last long. Landon followed me outside and I threw all common sense out the window. The guy has been getting under my skin since before we met, so I might as well kiss him in order to move on. Now here I am, assaulting his mouth with mine. *Way to exercise restraint, Dane.*

I need to savor this moment because it can only happen once. His lips taste sweet, his scent is so sexy, and everything about this kiss is turning me on. Still, after about ten seconds, I come to my senses and push him off. He looks at me in surprise, but I can't tell if it's good or not. I can't bear to watch him realize that I'm not really what he really wants, so I look down.

"There," I mutter, finally breaking the silence. "Now you can say you experimented. I hope you've gotten it out of your system." I look up to see his stare fixed on me. His eyes are darting all over my face, searching for something. I don't think I want him to find it. I turn to leave, but Landon grabs my arm.

"I'm not done," he announces roughly. This time, he's the one to bridge the gap between our lips. His mouth is demanding, and once again, my blood rushes down south. A moan escapes me, and my lips part, allowing his tongue to enter.

Our kissing becomes a delicious battle of dominance between mouths. It's been so, *so* long since I've properly made out with someone. I don't think kissing has ever felt this good. He nibbles on my lower lip, and his hands find my waist and hair. His moans are like a drug to me, fueling me to continue kissing him.

He brings his lips down to my neck, and I begin to pant. When I open my eyes, I remember that we're outside in public where anyone can see us—frankly I had forgotten we were on Earth. "Fuck, Landon," I groan as he continues to taste my skin.

"Do you want me to stop?" He's panting now too, and his voice is so deep.

"Someone…might…see us," I huff. He finally pulls off. His gaze is filled with concern and I notice how red his lips are.

"Do you not—" He's interrupted by the sounds of people walking by. Thankfully, it's no one we recognize. After looking around, we stare at each other again, then laugh. *Is this all seriously happening*?

"We should go get the others," I mutter, smiling. He nods and grins.

When we get back inside, we make up some excuse about me having a stomach ache, so Tisha, Jonathan, and Val agree to call it a night. Once again, Landon drives the five of us back to campus.

He drops off Jonathan and Tisha, then drives slightly farther to Val's dorm. I'm thankful I don't live in any of their buildings because I really want to wish Landon a special goodnight—and I do *not* want anyone around to witness that.

"I'm gonna park near the athletics dorms. Do you want me to drop you off somewhere?" He looks at me expectantly, and I think we're on the same page.

"I'll let you park first," I reply, trying to sound nonchalant. Landon's smirk is not lost on me.

Once he finally pulls into a spot, he turns off the engine and looks at me in the passenger seat. It's so quiet, and the tension between us is thick. Fuck, is it hot in here again? Landon really needs to fix this inconsistent heating situation because I am sweating.

I look over to see him looking up at nothing in particular, lips pursed like he's thinking of what to say. This is too awkward. I want to go, but I need to stay and say some form of goodnight.

"I just realized..." I begin slowly. He looks at me expectantly. "It's your birthday. I didn't get you anything."

"I disagree." Before I know it, he's reaching over and pulling my shirt collar in. Centimeters away from my face, he pauses. He's giving me an out, and I'm touched that he's being so thoughtful. I look at him and simply nod.

Our mouths meet, and suddenly it's an encore

performance of our tongues tasting each other. Landon must have some pheromones because I could breathe him in forever. My fingers explore his scalp while I try to memorize the way he tastes. I push his head up with both hands and he complies, knowing I want to taste his neck. I trace my tongue down to his collar bone and suck little marks into his skin up to his jaw. He moans in pleasure, so I know he's enjoying what I'm giving to him. Every part of him so far tastes good, and I wonder what his cock tastes like. Finally, I kiss my way back to his lips and we make out some more.

An eternity or five minutes later, we pull apart, panting. I smile and he grins back. "Good birthday?" I ask, breathing heavily.

"The best." His voice is deeper than usual and his eyes are glistening. I notice him looking down at my lips again. I need to call it a night before I let him fuck me right here in the campus parking lot.

"Glad to hear it. It's late though, I should get going."

"Alright." He smiles.

"Good night Landon." I open the car door and try to convince my erection to go down so I can walk in peace.

I hear him holler "Night, Dane!" as I close the door. I don't look back as I march away, because if I do, I'll end up back in his arms and on his mouth.

I'm starting to forget why that's such a bad idea.

15: Landon

Coach wants us to be in shape for Monday's game, so Sunday evening we work on calisthenics in the Athletics Center gym. It's a facility exclusively for team sports and staff, and today, the men's soccer team has it. Each of us on the team is working on a different exercise machine, lifting various types of weights.

I'm lost in thought as I go through the motions of my workout. *Dane kissed me, Dane kissed me, and it was awesome. Dane kissed me—Ahh!* Inside I'm squealing like a teenager who lost his virginity to the hottest girl in school. In a way, I kind of am a virgin. Dane is changing the way I see myself, the way I feel about men, and I don't dislike it. No, I'd say I love it.

As I swoon internally and replay the events from last night, I feel a hand stop me from pulling the weight machine bar down. I look over to see a tall mass of a man wearing a faculty uniform. It's Logan Micucci, the Athletics Center facilities manager. Every campus athlete knows and loves him. He's always offering guidance or shooting the shit with all of us. He can't be more than a few years older than me, and we all consider him to be one of the guys. Basically,

75

Logan is everyone's cool, older brother.

"You alright there man?" he asks.

"Uh, yeah." I try to pull myself out of thoughts of Dane's lips on my mouth and neck. "What's up Logan?"

"You seem distracted."

"What makes you say that?"

"You've been doing lat pull-downs with only 5 lb. of resistance for the last ten minutes." I look up to see that, indeed, I forgot to set the weight.

"He went out with his dance crew yesterday," Omar quips as he strolls by.

"Fuck outta here!" I reply, and Omar just giggles and walks away. "I'm fine."

Logan looks at me dubiously and I squirm under his perceptive gaze.

"Your first game is tomorrow. I know the spring season isn't as important, but Coach Dacks will have your head if you don't keep yours clear."

I nod and look down. "Yeah...Yeah, I know. I just…"

"Had a really good time last night?" I jolt upright and see Logan smirking with one eyebrow raised.

"Uh, uh…" I sputter.

He hands me a fresh hand towel and leans in to whisper, "You have a massive hickey on your neck. Put this on."

I feel my face get hot, and I immediately put the towel around my neck. Logan gives me a knowing nod and proceeds to adjust the weight of the machine. "Start with 35 lb. and work your way up!" he says loudly. "You know the drill by now."

"Yes sir," I reply with an easy laugh. Logan smiles and walks away.

"Hey, Kareem you better pick up that towel!" Logan

hollers and I'm relieved when I hear some of the guys laughing, knowing their attention is off me.

Everyone else leaves the locker room after practice, but I slowly tie my shoes and stay behind. I take extra time to zip up my hoodie to make sure the blue spot on my neck is no longer visible. After a minute, I see Logan pushing a linen cart in and approach him.

"Hey Logan. Thanks for um…" I point to my used towel and put it into the linen cart.

He smirks. "No problem Landee."

"You know my real name?"

"I know everything about the athletes. But your secrets are safe with me, young one," he says with a faux sternness. "I assume you had a date last night that you don't want the guys to know about?"

"Um…" I scratch the back of my head and look down.

"I recall you talking about girls nonstop last semester."

"Well, I'm trying something new." *Shit.* "I mean… personality-wise!" Fuck, I'm blushing again, aren't I?

Logan looks at me perplexed while locking up the linen cart. "Landon, isn't your best friend dating a guy?"

"Uh…"

"No one should be ashamed of whom they're dating. Your friends will accept you, I'm sure." He looks at me expectantly.

"It's…all just new."

"Fair enough."

"Thanks, though." I smile. Before I leave, I turn around one last time. "Hey Logan? How do you know if someone…likes you? And wants to date you?"

Logan shifts uncomfortably and looks up. "Considering

what's going on in my life, I am *not* the person you should be asking."

"Oh." I guess I'm getting too personal with him? He seems to be talking to himself here.

"But…I will tell you this: nothing will change unless you keep hanging out with him. Or her. Whoever."

I smile with relief and walk out of the locker room, looking forward to the next time I see Dane.

16: Dane

Monday during our small group dance class, I plug in my portable speakers to the outlet. The girls stand at the bar, waiting for my instructions. It feels like there's a gaping void where Landon usually stands, but we all know he has a soccer game today.

"I finally decided on the song for our semester showcase!" I announce. "We're going to dance to 'Try Again' by Aaliyah."

Tisha and Val look at each other, smiling with their eyebrows raised. "Wow, a real hip-hop dance song," Tisha remarks.

"Yup. I figured we can incorporate Latin movements for the first half, with hip-hop and modern for the second."

"I distinctly recall you only wanting to choreograph to orchestral music because it's 'more respectable.'" Val raises her hands with dramatic air quotes with those last words, and Tisha smirks.

"Yeah, well. I've been listening to a lot of R&B and hip-hop lately." I scratch my arm and look off to the side.

"I think Landon listens to that kind of music as well. Did

he give you the idea?"

"Maybe. I don't know." I put my foot on the barre and really focus on this stretch. This is a really important stretch so I can't look at the girls. That's totally the reason I'm avoiding eye contact.

"I remember asking you if we could do a hip-hop song at the beginning of the semester." I can hear Tisha grinning. "Maybe if I'd grinded on you on the dancefloor at the Mousetrap, you would've taken *my* suggestion." Val and Tisha are giggling even harder now.

"I...I don't know what you're talking about," I stutter, stretching my other leg. I have no doubt my face is red.

"We saw you two walk outside together. What happened?" I look up to see Val smiling.

"Nothing. We talked. Can we please start dancing now?" I sound flustered, completely giving myself away, but I don't even care.

"I'm sure you talked," Val snickers.

"Alright!" I stand between the two of them "We're going to start with a lean to the right, and all of our weight is on our right foot!" I lean my body, and the girls follow my instruction.

Maybe, if I'm loud and demanding enough during class, they'll forget all about my love life.

Two days later, we have our large group dance class, and it's the first time I'm seeing Landon since we kissed—and made out, and sucked on each other's necks in his car. I'm hoping to get him alone after class to chat, but during our water break, I hear him beg Professor Ryn to get out five minutes early for some soccer event. She obliges, of course, because athletes always seem to get their way at this school, but not before firmly telling him he needs to make up the rehearsals with me.

More one-on-one private dance classes with Landon? I don't know if I should laugh with relief or cry in frustration.

We're so engrossed with the different choreography during class that I don't have time to talk to him before he leaves class early. Shit, so much for my plan.

After class gets out, I'm lost in my memories as I walk to the student union. While I make my way to the QPU room, one thought stands out more than the others; Landon is avoiding me. It's possible that he's just busy with soccer, what with two games now in the past three days. Maybe I'm reading too much into it, or maybe he really is done with me.

Ugh, this shit is too frustrating. I liked it better when he was just an unattainable straight jock.

"Bullshit. You liked making out with him, and you want to do it again asap." Shut up, inner voice.

I need to stop talking to myself and process what I'm going through. I'm so lost in my head I don't even realize when I'm walking into the QPU room and nearly bump into Wei sitting at the desk.

"Oh," I say, waking myself up. "Hey Wei, I can take over 'Safe Space' now."

"Dane? You're not at 'Safe Space' today."

"I'm not?"

"No. It was in the group document." He turns his laptop to show me the online calendar we all work on together. "See? You're not here on Wednesdays."

"Oh." My face falls. I must have read the document wrong.

This just proves thinking about Landon constantly is detrimental for my health.

"It happens to the best of us." He smiles at me and I shrug. "You can stay if you want. I haven't had anyone all day, and it's been kind of boring."

"Um…" I look around and remember that 'Safe Space' is confidential. An idea begins to form. "Actually…Can I talk to you?" I close the door and look at him expectantly.

"Oh." His eyebrows jump. "OH!" He sits upright and puts his hands on the desk while I sit down. "Sure. Uh, right. Hi. My name is Wei, and—"

"Yeah, you can skip that," I interrupt him, waving my hand. He nods.

"Okay. Well, what did you wanna talk about?"

I look at him and sit upright. I need to be subtle and protect Landon's confidentiality. *Okay, here goes.*

"Remember that blond athletic guy who came in here a few weeks ago before me? Well, his name is Landon, he's on the school soccer team, and he's in the dance class I TA for. I kissed him last weekend at a club and he kissed me back but now I think he's avoiding me and I really like him and I don't know what to do!"

Well that was a failure.

I finally catch my breath after that word vomit, and Wei looks at me, eyebrows raised. "Uh…wow." He looks down like he's trying to process the little monologue I just gave him. "Okay. Well, what makes you think he's avoiding you?"

"He ran away early today after class for some soccer event."

"Do you usually see him multiple times a week?"

"Mondays he's usually in class, but he had an away game, I think."

"So either he's avoiding you, or he's legitimately busy with soccer."

"Oh." It makes way more sense hearing a real adult say this; I'm not sure why. "I guess that's...entirely possible."

Wei clicks on his computer. "Here. It says on the school website there's a men's soccer game going on right now."

"That must be the event." My heart is racing now.

"Anyone can show up, but I bet it would seem really supportive if he saw you there." Wei smiles and shrugs.

I smile back and get up. "Thanks, Wei. Hopefully we can chat and see where things go."

"Remember, making assumptions in your head won't help the situation. It sounds scary, but you should really consider talking things out with him. Let him know your concerns and how you feel about him."

"You're right. Thanks, again."

As I walk out the door, I swear I hear him mutter, "*I need to take my own advice.*" Maybe I'm just hearing things.

17: Landon

I usually look forward to the first home game of the season. The smell of the grass and getting to play my favorite game, even in the winter, brings me to life. However, I'm a bit distracted this year. I had to leave dance class early today, so I didn't get a chance to talk to Dane. He kept looking at me, expecting me to chat, but I couldn't keep up with the *piquée turns* and all the other fancy stuff the professor was teaching us. Before I knew it, it was time for me to run to the locker room.

The first half of the game is rough. While I enjoy starting and being on the field, the other team actually manages to check us in all of our plays. We stop them just as well, so the score is tied at a whopping zero. Coach Dacks has plenty to say to us in the lockers during halftime, and I try to pay attention. The gist of it is, I'm starting next half as well with some of the newer guys, in an effort to prevent the opposing team from anticipating our moves.

As I walk onto the field, I look in the stands and see one new person sitting right in the front. He's got a black hoodie and a red beanie hat, and I recognize his purple left eye. I smile and try not to freak out internally. Dane has never been to one of our games before, as far as I know. I wave and see him do the same.

I try to hide my smile and focus on the game. I might be blushing, but I don't even care. Tendrils of hope and anticipation are sneaking into my brain now. *Does this mean Dane wants to watch me play? I bet this means Dane likes me!* If I was a dog, I would be wagging my tail.

I focus on playing even better in the second half, and one of our freshmen, Paul, manages the one goal all game. We intend to give him plenty of pats, cheers, and noogies of affection in the locker room after.

Before we all leave to go change, I see Dane walking out in the stands. He looks at me and I wave. We're separated by some chairs and gates, but I manage to yell, "Meet me outside the Athletics Center?" I flail and point to where I'm going. He smiles and points back. This is a good sign, right?

Walking out of the building, I spot Dane instantly, leaning on a gate. He looks adorable, and I have a vision of grabbing him and kissing him, but of course, there are other people around, so I don't. Instead, I opt for a smile and raise out my fist for him to bump.

"Hey man, glad you made it!" He pounds my fist and returns my smile.

"Hey, glad to watch. It was awesome!"

"You really enjoyed it?"

"Yeah, for sure!"

"Not just because of all the hot guys on the field?" I give a dramatic wink and poke him with my elbow and he giggles.

"There *mayyy* have been one or two hot guys." He's rolling

his eyes but smiling.

"Really?" Is he flirting with me? I hope so. "Do tell."

Before he can respond, Kareem and Omar walk up to us and nod. "Dining hall?" Kareem asks.

"Bet. I'll meet you there." The others barely look at Dane before they walk away. I turn back to see him looking down. "Me and the guys are getting food right now. Games always make us hungry."

"It's cool." He looks up. Disappointment flashes on his face before he smiles. "I should get going."

"Come with us?"

"What?" He looks confused.

"Come with us to get food. Please," I whine. I want him to hang out and get to know me at school outside of messing up in dance class. "Pretty please."

He looks ahead at the guys walking away then looks back at me and nods. "Okay."

We start walking a decent distance away from the others up ahead. Hopefully we're out of earshot. "So what'd you think?"

"It was cool. I was trying to keep up. I've never seen one of these before."

"You're breaking my heart." Dane chuckles at this. "Speaking of disappointment, sorry I couldn't make it to dance class on Monday."

"No worries."

"I'm gonna make it up to you."

"Oh?" Dane grins and side-eyes me. "How so?"

"Private one-on-one sessions." I smirk and I swear I see him blush. It's so cold out I can see my breath, but walking with Dane keeps me warm somehow.

---

* * *

We take our time getting food at the late-night dining hall. By the time we pay, Omar and Kareem have a table far away from anyone else; not that many people eat at this late hour.

As I approach the table, I realize I have to introduce Dane. Shit, what do I say?

"Hey, um, this is my friend Dane. He was at the game." He waves at Kareem and Omar before sitting down. "Dane, this is Omar and Kareem."

"Hey," Dane says shyly.

"Sup." Kareem nods.

Omar however, stares at him with a distrustful expression. "Hey, are you that dance guy?"

"Yep," Dane says. "You talk about me?" His tone is teasing and I think my face is now beet red.

"I talk about all my classes." I shrug and try to nonchalantly drink my water.

"So," Omar says, eyes darting between me and Dane. "What are your intentions with our dear Landon?"

My eyes try to shoot laser beams at him, but Dane just laughs. "Nothing malicious I swear," he replies.

"That's too bad," Omar remarks. "This guy's ego needs to be taken down a notch."

"Word," Kareem adds, now grinning. I need new friends.

"Okay, well, let's talk about that *game!*" My voice is a bit louder than it needs to be, and the others all giggle at once.

"I'd rather get to know your friend," Omar says with a grin.

"I don't mind." I turn to see Dane smiling and chewing on a chicken finger, the traitor.

"So what does Landon look like while he's dancing?" Omar sounds so earnest, but I know he just wants fuel to roast me with later.

"He's actually pretty good." I turn to Dane. I don't know if he's lying to save my face or if he genuinely believes I'm a decent dancer. "Speaking of, he missed class on Monday 'cause of your away game. How'd it go?"

"Oh we did pretty well." Omar says. Kareem turns to him and pretty soon, the three of us are chatting soccer. You'd think the three of us would want to talk about anything else, but apparently we have a lot to say about the recent games.

At one point, I smile at Dane, silently thanking him. I know he changed the subject for my benefit, and I can't help but be smitten with how sweet that was.

18: Dane

It's getting late and we're all done eating, so I announce to these jocks that I'm peace-ing out. I live a bit farther than they all do, so I need to get walking.

"I'll walk with you to your dorm!" Landon blurts. I look at him puzzled. Why would he do that? His dorm is right next to the dining hall. "You know, so we can...talk about dance class."

Weird. I'm not sure why he's lying, but I wouldn't mind the company, so I shrug and wave off the others. Omar and Kareem give each other a funny look, but I don't know what it means.

We finally make it out of the building and I walk down the stairs. I've got my hands dug into my hoodie, and I'm still freezing. It's a typical Korham U winter night. Landon keeps up the pace next to me, and after a minute he finally breaks the silence.

"Don't mind my friends, they're just messing around."

"I thought they were cool." I reply candidly.

"Uh, sure. You know that reminds me, that building is

where I saw an advertisement for 'QPU Safe Space' for the first time?"

"Oh really? Well, good to know all those trees we killed went to good use." I realize I'm making dumb jokes just to ease the tension, but frankly, I still don't know why Landon is walking me to my dorm.

"Yup. 'Safe Space' is great. It was really…enlightening."

"Now you're just trying to flatter me."

"No, really! You helped me out a lot. Made me…realize things." It sounds like there's so much weight behind his words.

"Is that the *only* way I helped you come to terms with… your identity?"

"No." I can hear him smiling and I feel my face get warm. How is this guy still getting under my skin after all these weeks? The kiss was supposed to end it, and all it did was make me go to a freaking soccer game!

We finally make it to my building, and, after I swipe my key card, I hold the door open for him. Whatever we're doing, it won't be out here in the frozen tundra. He smiles at me, and I feel the butterflies in my stomach while he walks through the doorway.

"There's a lounge over here if you wanna talk." He follows me into the public lounge, and I'm glad no one else is here at this hour. Truthfully, I can't be trusted to keep my head straight if I invite him to my room.

Right now, I'm barely keeping it together as we both sit on a couch in the corner. I've still got my hands in my hoodie pockets to help resist the urge to grab his hand.

"I can't believe how cold it is tonight," Landon remarks.

"You're going to have to walk back through it to get to your dorm."

"I know." He smirks at me. This small talk is so awkward, but I really don't know what else to say.

After thirty seconds of silence, I say, "We don't have to hook up," right when Landon says in a much louder voice, "I wanna date you!"

We blurt out, "What?" at the same time. There is no way I heard him right.

Landon and I chuckle awkwardly. "You first," he says.

"Did you say you wanna date me?" I hope I don't come off as disgusted, I'm just trying to wrap my mind around it. It doesn't make sense.

Landon breaks out in a shy smile. "Yeah. If, uh, you want to..."

This has to be some sick joke. No one's ever asked me out before, but I'm not about to let that slip. "Aren't you still experimenting?"

"Nope. Kissing you confirmed that I am, in fact, very bi and very into you."

"I...I kissed you first." I'm trying to reason with Landon, make him realize that I am definitely not worth dating.

"And I kissed you second. And now I wanna date you."

"This has to be some weird prank." I get up and shake my head, turning to leave.

"It's not!" Landon yelps, getting to his feet. I turn and get a good look at him; he's so handsome, rich, and popular. Why would he want to date plain old, ugly me?

"I don't..." I'm not sure how I want to end this sentence. *Landon is asking me out. Why am I fighting this? This is exactly what I wanted!*

Landon leans in and slowly puts a finger on my chin, forcing me to look at him. "Pretty please?" He knows he has me wrapped around his finger.

"I...I think I need to think it over." I expect Landon to get mad at this, but instead he shrugs and smiles.

"That's fair." *Seriously?*

"Okay."

He lifts his hand and reaches for my chin. I stare at him, not blinking, waiting for him to touch me, but right before he makes contact, he pulls back.

"Alright, well, I should probably get back to my dorm." He scratches his head. "You have a good night, Dane." With one last smile, he turns and walks out of the lounge.

I'm left standing there, alone in the dark, more questions in my head than answers. Landon is into me, presumably for real. So why can't I accept it?

19: Landon

Saturday evening, I'm sitting on the suite couch in just my boxers. My feet are propped up on the coffee table while I watch TV and pluck potato chips off of my chest and into my mouth. What has become of me?

Oh that's right, I have a crush on this gorgeous, talented, dancer dude who hasn't decided if he likes me or not.

I frown as I eat another chip. Upon reflection, it's safe to say he's into me on some level. He kissed me first, after all, but he seems unsure if going out with me is worth it. I realize I'm some dumb new-to-being-queer jock, but I'd *gladly* make it worth his time. I would even formally come out if it meant getting to date him.

Ravi walks out of his room, putting on his coat. He looks at me and does a double-take, and I don't bother looking up.

"Hey Landon, are you alright?" he asks, sounding genuinely concerned.

"Peachy," I deadpan. He looks down for a moment then looks up, eyebrows raised.

"I'm headed to the union for a movie night with Steven."

"Cool."

"They're showing the new *The Forever Squadron* movie."

"Sure."

"Queer Pride Union is hosting it. I think 'cause one of the actors or characters is gay or something."

"Oh?" I try to sound neutral, but he's piqued my interest. A slight smile grows on Ravi's face, and he can read me like an open book.

"Yup. Unless I'm mistaken, the vice president, Dane, is hosting it. You know him, right?"

"Uh, yeah." I try to sound nonchalant while I throw away the rest of the chips. Shit, I'm a mess.

"You wanna come?"

"I guess I could." I try to sound casual, like I'm still debating it in my head. Ravi's grinning, no doubt seeing right through me.

"Get dressed. Wear something nice." He's shrugging too, trying to hold back a laugh. I don't even care. I need to clean myself up.

Twenty minutes later, I'm dressed in clean clothes and entering the union building. Ravi and I walk down the closest staircase. The basement floor has various rooms for student activities, and QPU is holding this event in the small café. The room is dark, and there are several couches with about twenty students sprinkled throughout. I spot one couch in the center near a projector and I see Dane sitting there; his couch has a vacant space—jackpot! Steven sits on the couch next to him, intently watching the movie and eating popcorn.

We walk in quietly so as not to disturb the other patrons.

Ravi sits next to Steven, and they kiss, of course. I plop down next to Dane and smile as he turns his head. He does a double-take, and his eyebrows jump. He's so cute.

"What are you doing here?" he whispers frantically.

"I'm just trying to watch a movie." I shrug for emphasis.

"But you've never come to our movie nights before!"

"Shh." I put my finger to my mouth and grin. "People are trying to watch."

Dane looks concerned and I smile. He finally relaxes back down into the couch to man the projector, and it thrills me to know I make him nervous. This is a good sign, maybe?

An hour and a half later, people are filing out of the café. I have no idea what happened in the movie; I was too busy focusing on Dane sitting *so close to me*. The entire time I was attuned to every movement he made, every little glance he sent my way. He kept fidgeting, and each motion sent little shock waves through my body from where he sat, seven inches away.

When I've gone to movies with girls, I was always planning on how to get to second base in the dark, and honestly, with Dane, the attraction is similar, yet so different. I want to touch him, to kiss him, but I'm not sure what else I'd be ready for. With girls, movies were means to one end—sex. With Dane, I want so much more.

With the lights on, I get up and take my time to stretch. I want to hang out with Dane just to talk, but there's still people around. It's so frustrating. *Everyone else needs to leave!*

"Hey, we're going to get food," Ravi says, turning to Dane and me. "Do you guys want to..." Steven gives him a weird look I can't interpret. "Uh...uh...want to...leave us alone?

Goodnight!" They both dash out of the café, and soon, it's just me, Dane, and a lot of empty popcorn bags.

I stand there looking at him expectantly. "I need to clean up," Dane mumbles, not looking me in the eye.

"I'll help!"

"You don't have to."

"I know, but it's...maybe a nice thing to do?" Dane smiles and shrugs.

"Okay," he replies quietly.

Soon enough, we're both cleaning in silence. We get into a groove of him picking up some litter, while I move the garbage can closer to him and pick up any other pieces of trash. I notice some paper buckets with popcorn in them still, so I take a kernel and toss it in the air, then catch it with my mouth. I hear Dane giggle one table over.

"You're good at that," he remarks with a smile.

"Yeah, well, athletics and shit." I toss another piece and catch it and chew.

"Wow, may I?" He motions that he wants to throw me one.

"Go for it," I reply, my eyes filled with challenge. He tosses a piece and I catch it and chew. He laughs and tosses another and I have to bend to the right, but I get it. "Ehh??" I smile.

He's full-on grinning now. I do so love making him smile.

Finally, there's nothing left to clean, so I sit back down on the couch next to the projector. Dane looks conflicted, but eventually he has a seat as well. Was it really only four days ago that we were in this exact position in his dorm?

"So..." he begins, tapping his fingers on his knee. I'm hearing him loud and clear.

I lift my hands and say, "Hey, we're in the union café. I promise I won't make a move. No funny business."

"Then what are we doing here?"

I turn to him and slide to get a little closer. "We're just... two friends, chatting. If that's all you want, I'm cool with it too."

His expression softens, and he looks down. After a few seconds he finally whispers, "I've never been asked out on a real date before."

"What?"

"I've never been—"

"I heard you but, what?" My eyebrows are raised in shock. "Dane, how? You're so...so..."

"Weird-looking?" He points at his left eye.

"Attractive!"

Dane sits up straight and stares at me, looking concerned. I want to reach out and hold his hand, to take all his insecurities away, but I hold back. As I gaze at him, he strokes his jaw then looks down.

"Fuck," he whispers. Is that a good thing? I'm not even breathing at this point. "Landon, you have to be 100 percent straight with me."

"That ship sailed when I kissed you." I smirk.

"I'm serious! You have to be honest."

"Okay."

"If you're not feeling it, or you wanna back out, you have to tell me."

Is he saying what I think he is? I want to leap up for joy. "Okay," I say, smiling.

"I do want to go on a date with you." He's smiling now, too. Hell yes.

"But," he starts, face turning serious. *Huh? No, no but's!* "We need to establish some ground rules."

"Okay." I nod.

"This isn't an experiment, Landon. I won't be some... sexual lab rat."

"I bet you'd look sexy in a lab coat, though," I say, my eyes trailing up and down his body.

"I'm serious! You need to realize you're not straight if we're going to date."

"I swear." I cross my heart with my finger. "You're not an experiment."

"And we can't tell anyone." I look at him confused. "It's not that I'm ashamed. It's just...this is really new, and I'm still your TA."

"Ah, got it."

"We can tell our friends later. If, *and only if,* we decide after a couple of dates that we want to pursue this. The beginning of possibly, eventually...you and me...being a...you know... thing..."

He's so cute when he babbles. I take his hand in mine on the couch and interlace our fingers. "I very much would like to pursue us possibly being a thing." I can't help but lean in, grinning.

"You know," he says, voice getting deep. "I have this room for another hour or so."

"Oh really? What did you want to do, Mr. Poorweisz?" I wag my eyebrows at him. At this point, I'm down to hook up on school property. I don't even care who walks in.

"Let's make this our first date!" He bolts upright, smiling, and I fall back on the couch.

"Huh?"

"I can hook my phone up to the projector. We can watch something together."

"Okay." I stand up, still confused.

"Why don't you go get us some food?" He leans in closer to

me, putting one finger into my front pocket. What a tease. "Then after we've eaten, we can prop our feet up and sit on the couch...together?" His eye looks at me expectantly.

I like the sound of that.

"Bet." I grin and walk out of there.

Twenty minutes later I return, huffing from running with all this food in hand. "I got chicken fingers and french fries from the late night dining hall." It's just dawning on me that it is not appropriate first date cuisine. I feel like an idiot.

"Yes, my favorite!" Dane squeals in delight as he helps me put the food on a table.

We sit and eat and chat about nothing important. Just like on our car rides, talking to him is so easy. He's chill with me, like a bro, but he means so much more.

"Okay, so," Dane says as he wipes his face. "For entertainment, we can watch *American Dad* or *Community*. I have them both queued up on my phone."

"Wow, excellent options. Why not both? Back-to-back episodes."

"Deal." The smile Dane gives me sends those butterflies back down, and I'm pretty sure they're going to need to start paying rent if he sticks around.

And you really want him to stick around. I don't even mind my inner voice today.

Pretty soon, *American Dad* is playing on the projector. At least I think it's playing. Once again, I can't concentrate. We're back on the couch, but the few inches that separated us during the movie are gone. Dane has taken my left arm and wrapped it around himself, cuddling up against my shoulder. He's so warm, and the stubble on his face reminds me that he's nothing like the girls I've done this with. Yet, this feels right;

before, cuddling was just a means to get laid. Now? I could curl up with Dane for hours, and I'd never want to let go.

I pull him close, and he lifts his chin, turning to look at me with his good eye. "This okay?" I ask, tugging him in tighter.

"It's great," he replies, his voice barely a whisper, and then puts his head back down. It's more than that. It's perfect.

After we watch an episode of *Community* and laugh our asses off, I help Dane put away the projector and lock up. We throw away our trash and head out. I'm not ready for this night to end yet, and I think Dane is on the same page.

I throw my arm around him as we walk out the doors. "So what do you wanna do now?" It's beginning to snow, and the cold night sky makes everything feel so surreal, like we're in a snow globe or something. "We could go back to my place to watch more shows."

"I think I'd like that, going back to your place." He stops, pulls my arm off, and turns to look at me. His face is suddenly serious, and it's like he's trying to interpret something. "Your room is nice and private, right?"

"Yeah," I reply, still not sure what he's getting at. "You wanna chill in my room to watch TV on my phone?"

"I wanna chill in your room." He leans in to whisper into my ear. "*And not watch anything.*"

At this, I swear I can hear the '*whoosh*'-ing noise of all the blood going straight into my cock.

20: Dane

I'd be lying if I said I'm not nervous right now. Landon took me home with him at the end of our fantastic impromptu date. I can see myself cuddling up with him and watching TV regularly for a very long time to come. It just feels right to be in his arms. I've had sex with guys, but random internet hookups rarely want to cuddle with the twink with the messed-up eye.

Now, I'm walking up to his suite, and I'm trying not to freak myself out. There's still plenty of voices in my head telling me this is a prank, Landon is lying, and he could never care for someone like me. I've only gotten hurt in the past. It's true that he might break my heart one day, but tonight? Tonight I want his body, and I want mine to be his.

We walk into the suite and notice Omar, eating popcorn in the common room, eyes glued to the TV. He barely acknowledges us—he must be really interested in whatever movie he's watching—and Landon guides me to his room, putting his finger on his mouth to tell me to be quiet. I try not to laugh as he unlocks the door.

His room is small but clean. There are some soccer posters

on the wall, and a computer on the desk, a typical dorm. He starts moving random clothing items into the closet and the hamper. He seems nervous, and that calms me down a notch.

"Can I just sit anywhere?" I ask quietly.

"Yeah just um… I have a chair and…" Hell no. I push the covers over, kick off my shoes, and sit down on the bed . It's elevated, so I do a little jump to get there. I'm sitting down with my back against the wall, feet dangling, but Landon is still refusing to make eye contact. He seems preoccupied with tidying up. I clear my throat, and he whips his head around. He looks nervous, so I give him a reassuring smile and pat the bed next to me, wiggling my feet for good measure.

"Oh, um, should I turn off the lights?" There's one desk lamp that illuminates half the room, so we can see each other clearly.

"If you want."

"What do you want?" He smiles at me. How considerate of him.

"Keep it on." I shrug. "I like looking at you." I give a devilish smirk, and it seems to tickle him.

He finally crawls into the bed and sits on the wall next to me, our shoulders touching. "So…" Landon says. He's twiddling his thumbs and looking at the ceiling. Poor thing, I need to make him not nervous. It's evident I'm going to have to take the lead, which is understandable.

"Landon." He looks at me. "I kinda wanna continue what we did last Saturday in your car. If that's okay."

He nods and grins. I lean in slowly, bringing my hand to his jaw. He leans in as well, and a moment later, his lips are on mine. We kiss gently this time. This is new territory for us —a recurring theme for tonight. There's no urgency, no pent-up frustration, no grabbing of collars; we're kissing softly, like the other person is a delicate flower. Just like before, it feels fantastic, and so, so right.

My reasons not to date Landon fade away with every moment I spend kissing his lips.

Soon enough, our kisses get stronger, tongues entering into play, and I feel my blood start to race. My hands venture to his muscular chest and his do the same. Then, my arms get lower, snaking around his waist, and I feel my body begging for more. *More contact, more kissing, more everything.* Except for clothes, we need less of those.

I start to frantically undo the buttons on his shirt while he moves down to kiss my neck. After way too long, I manage to push it open, and I pull back to look down and— *damn.* I knew he was an athlete, but his abs are deliciously tight. He pries the shirt right off and asks, "Is this okay?" As if I'm going to say no to this sexy guy who's always getting under my skin.

"Hell yeah," I grunt, out of breath. I jump off the bed, and it takes me about ten seconds to strip down to my black briefs, which now barely restrain my hard dick. I look up and see Landon, frozen in the act of removing his pants while on the bed. "Is everything alright?"

"Yeah, I just wanna… look at your for a little bit." He's staring at me, open-mouthed, and I am flattered to the moon and back.

I leap back on the bed onto his side and kiss his neck. "Let me help you," I moan as I tongue behind his ear. I undo his zipper and push down his pants. I maneuver to the side so he can get up, and in one sweep, the pants and boxers are down. Hallelujah.

He jumps back in the bed and begins to stroke his hardness. *Oh no you don't.* I bat his hand away and kiss him down his chest. I lick each nipple, and I'm rewarded with a quiet, little yelp. As he moans, my mouth moves down to my target. I make it to his chiseled thighs and give each a wet kiss. He falls back onto the pillow, panting. Then, finally, I stroke his dick, and he squirms and groans.

"Landon, I wanna make you feel so good." I kiss his thighs some more but I never stop slowly stroking him. He nods in response, his eyebrows raised. "Can I make you feel good with my mouth?"

He nods, biting his lip, and I finally do what I've been wanting to do for weeks now. I get to give Landee Landon, soccer player, his first taste of oral sex from another guy. I take him in, and he falls back onto the bed. His penis is so smooth, and he's not too large, so I happily give my throat a workout.

I love giving head, but this is so much more. His eyebrows are furrowed, and his jaw has gone slack, like he's having an existential crisis. In a way, he is, and I intend to resolve it. I suck and stroke and get his dick so wet, using my tongue right underneath the cock head, where all guys like it. I might not ever get another shot at this, so this blowjob has to be one for the record books.

"I'm gonna…" He whimpers, his voice rising an octave. His abs quiver, his strong soccer player thighs clutch the sides of my face, and he unloads into my mouth. I take it all in, and I'm overjoyed knowing I got to do this for Landon.

After he's done using my mouth as a sperm donation cup, I look up to see him lying back, mouth open. He looks so blissed out that I'm once again flattered, but I'm mostly horny. I shimmy out of my briefs and lie next to him. There's barely any room but I start stroking myself off.

He opens his eyes and looks at me like he just remembered what planet he's on. "Do you…Do you want me to—" Before he can finish that sentence, however, I come right there at the sight of his naked body. I moan as ropes of semen splash onto my abs. I think I pass out for two minutes after.

When I open my eyes again, I see Landon using a towel to gently clean me off. It's a simple act, but it feels so intimate, like he's really taking care of me even though we both already got off. The next thing I know, he flicks the light off and curls up next to me, pulling the sheet over us.

"So...I got to take your 'first date virginity.'"

"Yup." I'm smiling now. "And I got to take your 'gay oral sex virginity.'"

"Yup." We both giggle. "And it was perfect."

I drift off to sleep with Landon kissing my shoulder, whispering something about 'perfection.' I don't know what he says. The last thing I remember is thinking I could easily get used to this.

21: Landon

It's early on a Sunday morning, so it's easy for me to sneak Dane into our suite bathroom without being seen. After I'm done using the toilet—I use a little mouthwash too—I ditch my clothes and hop back in bed as I direct him on where to go. When he returns from the bathroom, I open the blanket beckoning him to jump back in bed. It's still early, and I just want to cuddle with him some more. For a moment, I think he's going to refuse, but he ditches his pants and hops back in — score!

Spooning Dane in the early morning hours feels almost as good as the sex from last night—and that's saying a lot. His body is so toned, with smatterings of hair in all sorts of places. Still, none of this feels weird. Turns out there's nothing weird about sleeping with a guy; maybe I've just been sleeping with the wrong people all these years.

Eventually, he rolls onto his back and I curl onto his chest. He rubs my back and we just lazily let the sunrise wash over us. I listen to his heartbeat, and my toes play with his. It's like we're in this bubble, the snow globe from last night, and once he walks out that door, it's back to us being the jock and his dance TA.

When it's almost eight, Dane finally breaks our comfortable silence. "How was that for a first time?"

"Amazing." I want to be honest with him so I continue. "But if we're talking first times, *technically* you're not my first kiss with a guy."

"Oh really?"

"Yeah. As a freshman, one of the soccer seniors dared me to kiss Kareem at a party."

Dane chuckles, his chest vibrating through me. "And how was that?"

"Honestly? It was part of the reason I had no idea I could be gay or bi or whatever. Like, I felt *nothing*. Of course, I acted disgusted and Kareem didn't care."

"So it was weird?"

"Yeah, it was weird. Like putting my mouth on a piece of plastic. It was nothing compared to kissing you. Kissing you feels friggin' amazing." I smile into his side.

"You swear you're no longer experimenting?"

"Yes. I'm done."

"You're done?" He sounds so vulnerable. I look up at him to see him already looking down, worry etched on his face.

"Yeah. I'm done. With the experimenting." I smile at him. "But I'm not done with you." I lean up and kiss him gently, hoping his fears will fade away.

"Good," Dane says once I pull back. He pulls me in tighter. "But if you decide you don't want guys anymore, then..."

"Hey, you can't get rid of me that easily!" I chuckle and kiss his neck. "But we should probably discuss what happens once we walk out of this room though."

"Right." He nods and looks down in concentration. "Dance class has to remain professional."

"I wasn't gonna tell my friends yet." I flop onto my back and look over at him. "It's just...new, you and I. We're still feeling our way through. Besides, they'll probably ask to go on double dates and shit and I don't want to, not yet. I want my Dane all to myself."

I see him staring at me like I just gave him bad news. Before I can ask, he leans over and kisses me hard. Damn, I'll never get used to that.

"Deal. We keep it under wraps for now." He kisses me one more time, then gets out of bed. "I should get going, though."

"We'll do this again next Saturday right?" He looks at me and his eyebrows jump as he pulls up his pants.

"If you want." He sounds shy, but I'm not sure why. I get up and snake my arms around his bare torso.

"I very much want, Dane Poorweisz. I want to take you out on a date again, and again, and again."

"Okay." He smiles at me. "If you're busy or change your mind, that's cool too." He shrugs, trying to act like it's not a big deal.

I smooch the back of his neck and he giggles. "I already told you," I mutter into his skin, "you can't get rid of me that easily." Now that I've had a taste of Dane, I can't get enough.

We swear that dance class won't get affected, so I agree to meet with him Monday before class. We're practicing just the two of us in one of the side rooms so I can catch up on what I missed. Apparently, I shouldn't miss class anymore, because Dane's choreography is kicking my ass.

"Five, six, seven, eight," he announces. He claps while I attempt the moves he taught me not even fifteen minutes ago. It's tough and frustrating, but I think that's part of what I like about Dane. When we first met, he thought I was a talentless dumbass, but now he really wants me to excel at the routine. He doesn't see me as inept; he challenges me to be better.

Unfortunately, I'm not quite there yet.

"Uh, okay, that's..." His voice trails off while he nods at me, like I'm a toddler who fell off a two-wheeler. "Well, let's just do it again."

"Sorry," I whine, spinning around on my heel. "It's like my left arm won't work while I'm concentrating on where my feet go." I frown at him.

"Let's just take it from the top. It's not a dance class if we're not hitting the moves over and over." He shrugs. He's trying to comfort me, and I appreciate it.

"Can we take a break?"

"No Landon, we have a lot to cover! Class starts in fifteen minutes and I promised I wouldn't treat you any differently." It's only the two of us in the room, so I take that as a challenge.

"Not even if I make it worth your while?" My voice is deep while I walk two fingers up his chest to his neck. He's rolling his eyes, but he's smiling and hasn't tried to move away.

"Landon."

"Pretty please." I move my hand over his shoulder and sneak my left hand under his shirt.

"You think you can just get whatever you want from me every time you say those two magic words?" He's grinning, now and his face is getting redder.

"Now you're catching on to my diabolic plan." I lean in close, my breath dancing on his face. I want to kiss him so bad.

Right before I get to, I nearly topple as he pushes me back. Before I can ask him what the hell that was, I see his face. He looks like he's seen a ghost. I turn around to see Professor Ryn walking through the room and picking up a desk chair.

"Sorry, didn't mean to interrupt." She's not looking at either of us, but we're the only ones in the room. "Someone moved my damn desk chair. Carry on!" She walks out holding the chair, but she doesn't make eye contact at all. Did she see us?

"Uh…" I turn to Dane, cringing. "So…"

"Shit, she definitely saw us," he whispers. Fuck, is he upset?

"Um, it'll be okay."

"Let's just…keep practicing." He looks down, dejected. I don't want him to freak out, so I do what he says. I continue to repeat the choreography, still failing miserably most of the time.

Dane doesn't even look me in the eye while he goes through the moves. He sounds like he has a million other thoughts right now. I keep forgetting his credits are contingent on Professor Ryn, and that hooking up with a student is a no-no, even for TA's. Eventually, we both stop moving, and he leans on the barre in silence.

"Dane?" I ask gently, not wanting to upset him more.

"I'll talk to Ryn after class. I'll tell her it won't happen again."

"Okay," I reply quietly. But no, it's not okay.

Fuck. What does this mean for us?

22: Dane

After class, I tell Landon I'll meet up with him later because I need to talk to Professor Ryn. "I'll, uh, wait for you outside," he says, concern etched on his face. I wait for everyone else to leave before I approach Ryn. She's sitting on her desk chair, and she's booted up her PC.

"Hey." I clear my throat. "Can I talk to you professor?"

"Sure, what's up Dane?"

"Great class today. You know I enjoy doing *tour jetés*!" I chuckle, but she just nods and continues scrolling on her PC.

"Mhm."

"Right. Um...About what you saw in the practice room before class. Me and Landon... we were just joking around."

"Sure, no problem, just fill out the form," she replies casually, as if I'd asked her for a stick of gum.

"What form?"

"The form that says a TA and a student are in a relationship and there won't be a conflict of interest."

What? I'm dumbfounded by her response or lack thereof rather. "I don't...We're not in a relationship."

111

She finally looks up at me, her chin on her hand. "Dane, you know I trust you right?"

"Yes?"

"I've worked with you for years. I know you're not going to go easy on Landon just because you two have...relations, or whatever. I'm still the professor, and I still hand out the grades. You're a hard worker, and I can see that he's learning a lot from you. I know you won't let your romantic relationship affect your performance, both as a TA and as a dancer."

"We're not...in a relationship." I'm still trying to wrap my head around this whole conversation.

Ryn rolls her eyes and closes the PC. "With the way that boy looks at you?"

"I swear we're not!"

"Okay, sure." She looks at me, unconvinced. "Still, just go to the school website and print and fill out the form for me, please. I don't want anyone to get in trouble." She proceeds to walk out of the dance room and my feet are glued to the floor. I hear her shout in the hallway, "I'm watching you soccer boy!"

I shake my head and, after a moment, scramble out the door to see Landon waiting for me. He looks mortified.

"What happened?"

"I was gonna ask you," he whispers, frantically. No one's around. It seems Ryn has left.

"She told me to promise that our"—I point to the two of us —"isn't going to affect our performances. But otherwise, I think she's cool with it."

Landon breathes a sigh of relief and leans on my shoulder. "Wow. Okay. I'm glad. I thought you were going to break up with me already." He looks up and smiles at me. He's so cute, and it touches me to know he's invested in our budding relationship.

"We need to be more careful, though." I cup his cheek and kiss him quickly.

"Aye aye, sir." He winks and gives me a salute. "I gotta run to practice."

"Alright."

"Wanna quickly jerk off together first?"

"No! You have practice!" We're both giggling now. I turn his shoulders around and give him a hard slap on the ass. "Now get out of here!" I hear his laughter echo as he dashes down the hall.

The next day our class schedules don't sync up, so I don't get to see Landon at all. I assume I'm going to see him at class on Wednesday, but tonight I'm in the QPU room. We have our weekly meetings where we host a casual discussion about current events, usually LGBTQ-themed. These meetings are open to anyone, queer and allies alike, and they typically devolve into all of us hanging out at the end of it.

Today's topic is "*LGBTQ representation in Superhero media*" in order to coincide with our showing of *The Forever Squadron*. We're highlighting that there's an openly gay character as one of the main heroes. Because of this, I'm turning on a slideshow of comic book images as people file into the room.

"Hey Dane!" I look up to see Steven walking in, holding hands with Ravi. I smile back, but before I can greet them, I see someone else and my face falls. Landon is behind them.

I stare at him in shock as he greets me. "Sup man?" His cocky grin is giving me a weird mixture of horror and arousal.

"Uhh... hey?" I'm sure I sound freaked out. What is Landon doing here? I know anyone is allowed, but he's never been up here for a meeting before!

Steven and Ravi share a knowing smile and take a seat, with Landon sitting down next to Ravi. As vice president, I have to sit up front. More people start trailing in, and this week we have a turnout of about fifteen people. Pretty soon, Dominic starts the weekly discussion.

"So," he says in a booming voice. "This week we're going to play a trivia game called '*Name that Queer Comic Book Character.*' Dane, next slide please." I shake my head, chasing away my thoughts and click.

After the weekly discussion, we're all chilling out, as is customary for these types of meetings. The board games and video games are out, and clusters of people are gathered together, no doubt gossiping about the weekly happenings at the university. I'm leaning on the desk next to Dominic as we chill and play a Christina Aguilera song. I sneak looks at Landon, who's standing around watching Ravi and Steven play a video game. His frequent side glances my way are not lost on me, but we're trying to be discreet. Why he came to this meeting, then, is beyond me.

"He's hot," Dominic remarks, sipping on a juice box.

"Uhh, who?" I ask, my eyes shifting downward. The floor is really interesting all of a sudden. Dominic scoffs.

"I can't believe you and Steven *both* scored hot soccer jocks."

"I don't...uh..." It's hard to lie to Dominic. He's as perceptive as they come.

"I'm happy for you, man, but I'm so jealous." He crunches his juice box and tosses it in a trashcan.

"I don't know what you mean." I'm fiddling with my thumbs and still having a staring match with the floor.

"So you're telling me that hot guy over there who's been throwing you '*do-me*' eyes all night isn't the guy Val told me about? The one you have angry sexual tension with in dance class?" Dominic is grinning and my face is getting hot.

"Um, now that you mention it, yes, he's in my dance class, but I don't...uh..."

"Oh, still trying to hide it?" He grins at me, a challenging look. "Alright. If you're not fucking around with him, then he's definitely not gonna walk over here." He leans in close to whisper in my ear. "Especially if I do this."

He places his hand on the other side of my face and kisses me dramatically on the cheek. I'm annoyed and roll my eyes, but Dominic and I are tight; we kissed each other as a joke all the time last semester. Right on cue, Landon appears next to me.

"Hey, hey...Hey Dane! What uh What's going on here? What's up? What's going on?" I push Dominic away and get a good look at Landon. He looks like he's having a panic attack.

"Nothing, Dominic was just being a weirdo." I sound aggravated, and Dominic is trying to hold back a laugh.

"Yeah, buddy, you shouldn't kiss people without their consent." Landon is starting to sound genuinely angry, so I put my hand on his shoulder and get between them.

"Don't worry Landon. It's nothing serious. Dominic is my good friend and a friendly asshole." I slap the back of Dominic's head and it sets off a massive cackle out of the guy.

"I'm sorry," Dominic huffs, tears forming from laughter. "That was...I promise that was nothing. Ooh, I needed a good laugh. I'm gonna go find my own hot jock to date, bye guys!"

I guide Landon out of the room and we walk to a corner in a hallway where no one's around. Once we find a bench, I sit both of us down and stroke his arm in an effort to get him to stop frowning. "That's just Dominic. We make jokes like that all the time. He's like a brother to me, or a pet teddy bear or something."

"I don't like that he was kissing you," Landon grumbles, still frowning.

"Please don't be mad at me." I smile and stroke his arm some more.

"I'm not mad at you. It's him I don't like."

I swoon internally. No one's ever been possessive of me before. He's so freaking cute when he's jealous. "Look, he's just a good friend. I promise you he's not interested in me."

"Good," Landon mutters as he rests his head on my shoulder. "I don't like anyone else kissing you but me."

"That sounds a bit exclusive-y when we haven't even had our second date." At this, Landon stiffens and he frowns. I rub his back and say, "I promise, I'm not kissing or dating anyone other than you."

Landon smiles and I swoon again. I make a mental note that I want to keep making him smile as often as possible. "You better not, Poorweisz." He kisses me quickly and then places his head on my shoulder. I rub his back and I find that I like comforting Landee Landon.

23: Landon

Saturday night is the big date night. While I enjoyed our impromptu first date, I really want to impress Dane tonight. When he texts me he's on the way down, I step out of my car. After a moment, I spot him, and he takes my breath away. He's got on a black blazer and a white button-down shirt. His eye sparkles when he gets to me.

"What's this?" Dane asks, grinning.

I look down and remember that I'm holding a singular rose in a paper bouquet wrap. I shake my head and reply, "It's for you!"

Dane blushes and smiles, his eye continuing to sparkle. "You...you didn't have to do that."

"Well, I wanted to."

"No one's ever given me flowers before."

"I hope you like it."

"I do. You're...so sweet, Landon. Thank you." I open up the passenger seat and he gets in.

As I drive downtown, I look over to see Dane already smiling at me. "You look...really good tonight."

I'm sure I'm blushing as his gaze travels over my body. I've got on a dark blue blazer and a green polo underneath. "Thanks. You look sexy as well. I mean, uh, handsome." I shake my head and frown as Dane snickers at me.

Sometime later, we're seated in the back of Marino's, the fanciest nearby Italian restaurant I know—within an undergrad's budget. There's a checkered table cloth and some olive oil and spices in front of us. The dark lighting sets a romantic mood and the illusion of privacy, but the lamp above our table lets me clearly see my date.

I'm on a fancy date with Dane, score! We give our orders to the waiter and settle into a comfortable silence. He smiles at me —he's gorgeous—and I smile back.

"Do you like it here?" I ask.

"Yeah it's really nice, friendly atmosphere, and I'm sure the food is amazing."

"It is. I've been here many times."

"On dates?" My shoulders stiffen as I look down.

"Um…Yes."

"It's no big deal, Landee. Everyone has a past." His tone is teasing, but he puts his hand on mine and I look up at him. This makes my heart beat faster. He lifts up his water glass with his left hand and declares, "To new beginnings."

I grin and lift my glass "To turning over new leaves." We clink glasses and each take a sip.

After putting his glass down, his face turns serious. "Um, this is going to sound weird."

"What?"

"You keep saying 'new leaf' but…it's like you're apologizing." I look down uncomfortably. If I ever want Dane and me to be...a thing... I need to be open and honest. "Landon?"

"Yeah." I clear my throat. "I've done some things...that I'm not proud of."

"You don't have to tell me if it makes you uncomfortable."

He's being considerate, but I continue. "It was actually right here." I look up at the light above me. "Here at Marino's. Last semester, I assumed Ravi was straight and I kind of forced him to go on a double date with me and two girls."

"Okay." He sounds nonjudgmental as always, so I keep going.

"Steven found out, and they got in a huge fight. Almost broke up and everything."

"Shit, he was dating Steven at the time?"

"Apparently. My best friend had a boyfriend, but I'm such an idiot I didn't realize it." My throat is dry so I take another sip. "For years I lived in a bubble, only seeing what I wanted to see. People saw me as an obnoxious loud-mouth, and I kind of stayed that way. I was just the worst."

I finally look up to see Dane; his face is filled with concern. He puts his hand back on mine and strokes his thumb across it.

"You're not an idiot, and you're not the worst," he says quietly. I smile, hoping my eyes tell him all the things I can't articulate.

"Thanks." I look down and keep going. "You say that, and it's sweet of you. But I was such a prick at times. I said shit about gay people that wasn't cool. I chased after girls I didn't care about. Worst of all, I hurt Ravi, my best friend. He means the world to me. The three of them are like my brothers."

Dane squeezes my hand. "For what it's worth, Ravi has

forgiven you. I can tell. He told me you're actually a good guy, that was right after we met and I was awful to you."

"Oh, right. You know them from Queer Pride Union."

"Yeah. And you're not a prick. You're thoughtful. And I..." Dane hesitates and looks down at his hands. "I'm glad you made it here."

I lift his hand and kiss it. "I'm really glad to be here, with you."

After dinner, neither of us is ready to go back to campus, so I suggest we take a walk. The night is still young, and the downtown street is surprisingly busy with patrons. It's a little cold since winter is far from over, but when Dane takes my hand and interlocks his fingers with mine, my whole body gets warm. Even though we're not headed anywhere in particular, with him by my side, I never feel like I'm lost.

Eventually we come upon a massive crowd going in and out of a building, just over a pedestrian bridge.

"Wanna head in? See what the commotion is about?"

"Sure," Dane replies.

We walk into a place called the Riverside Gallery. "Oh, this is a gallery opening! I've been here before."

"Really?" Dane asks as he walks through the door I'm holding open.

"Yeah. I came here last semester with Ravi for...Well, it's a long story."

We notice a spread of snacks and wine at the front table. Fortunately, it's a free gallery opening, so we don't have to pay. We walk down the right side to see various paintings, with subjects ranging from nude bodies to mountainous landscapes. I watch Dane's eyes widen in wonder as he looks at the works on the wall, noticing the way the light catches his beautiful face.

Suddenly, I feel him stiffen and pull apart our hands. I miss the contact immediately, but before I can ask what's wrong, I turn to my left and see Steven across the room. He makes eye contact with us, and his smile drops into a look of confusion. It's time to face the music, so to speak.

"Hey guys." Steven is walking over, and his eyes are darting between the two of us like he's trying to solve a math equation.

"Steven, hey." I greet him with a fist pump, and Dane uncomfortably does the same. "What brings you here?"

"I'm supporting my professors' artwork. What uh…" His eyes won't stop darting between the two of us. "Did you guys…come here together?"

Dane turns to me as if waiting for my cue. Fuck it. "Um… Yeah. We came here. Together." I take Dane's hand again and interlace my fingers with his. Now my hand is exactly where it belongs. He looks down in shock before looking back up at me, a slow grin spreading across his face. "We are here, together," I declare with confidence, my chin held high.

"Ah." Steven's eyebrows shoot up; he's full on grinning. He looks like he just found out Santa Claus is real. "Well, I don't want to interrupt. I hope you two have a great night." His tone is laced with innuendo but I don't even care. We smile and bid him farewell before walking to the other side of the gallery.

"Are you cool with that? You know he's a direct ear to Ravi?"

I shrug in response. "Let them talk. They might give me shit, but they'll need to get used to the idea of the two of us. I'd like to keep seeing you." A sudden nervousness overtakes me. "If you want to? Keep dating, that is."

This seems to be the right answer as Dane leans in to kiss me on the cheek, right here in front of everyone. "So far, I have to say I'm enjoying dating you very much, Mr. Landon."

24: Landon

Once we get back to campus, Dane suggests we go back to his dorm room—he has a single—so we can just hang out and talk. I'm really hoping that's code for what I think it is, but I'm willing to just hang out as well. Lately, chatting with Dane is the highlight of most of my days.

We're walking up the stairs laughing as I recount my misadventures from last semester. "How fast was Paul's dad driving?" Dane asks.

"At least eighty miles per hour," I chuckle as Dane unlocks the door. "And all the while, we're using markers to write big letters on poster boards!" At this, Dane laughs harder, and it makes me feel warm and fuzzy.

I walk in and look around. The walls of his room are barren, and there's no private bathroom, but otherwise it's nice and spacious. The window seems to open up to nothing but trees in the dark of the night. It's a wide room and Dane has all of this space to himself. I've never been in a single before, but something about it feels comfortable.

"Wow, nice place." I whistle and sit down on one of the two chairs near the bed.

"Yeah. It's one of the advantages of having a malformed eye. They had an extra single room for 'handicapped' students and technically I qualify."

"Wow, I didn't even realize that was a thing."

Dane hangs up his jacket, puts the rose on his desk, and moves the other room chair closer to me. He takes a seat, smiling right at me, our knees almost touching.

I want to make a move, but I need to ask him something first. "Do you often get special treatment 'cause of your eye?"

Dane's smile falls. Shit, did I trigger him? "Not typically. *Special* treatment? No." He looks down then scratches his cheek. "Treated *differently* well…Yeah, all the time."

There's so much pain he's hiding, but I can only imagine how hard it must have been. I don't tell him any of this. Instead, I put a hand on his knee. "I'm sorry if anyone treated you poorly. You don't deserve that. You're talented, charming, and amazing." Dane puts his hand on mine, then stares right at me. The single lamp in the room is barely illuminating his face, but he's still the most handsome person I've ever seen.

I want Dane to know I genuinely care for him. I want him to forget that anyone ever treated him like he's a lesser person just because his face isn't symmetrical. I want his pain to go away. I want him to feel good about being with me. I need to make Dane mine.

He slowly cups my cheek, then I lean in, putting my lips on his. Kissing him feels just as electric as the first time. I open my lips and slide my tongue against his. He tastes so good and I can't help but run my fingers through his hair. Blood flows downward, my skin feels hot, but I don't want to stop kissing for a moment. On some unseen cue, we both stand up, our hands finding the other's hips, our mouths never parting.

After making out for another minute, we finally part for air. I lick and nibble down his neck and he moans back sounds of approval.

"What do you...want to do...Landon?" Dane gasps as I suck on his lower neck.

"What do *you* want to do?" I murmur against his skin. He smells so deliciously *Dane* that I can't help but start to undo the buttons on his shirt.

"I was kind of pushy last time, so please tell me," he whines, still not stopping me from undressing him. I caress both his nipples at once and I'm gifted a high pitched moan. *Fuck yeah.*

"I want." I kiss lower, between his pecs. "To make you feel good." His shirt is undone, and I kiss down his perfect abs. "With my mouth." I lick the hair just below his belly button and he moans and squirms just a little bit.

On my knees, I graze his hard-on through his pants with my hand. I look up and see him moaning into his fist, his eyes screwed shut. I need him to relax. "Dane." He looks down at me. "I want your cock in my mouth."

His eyebrows jump, like he just discovered a glorious secret. I take that as approval, so I slowly undo his belt and I unzip him even slower, drawing it out to tease him. When I finally pull his pants and boxer briefs down, his hard cock springs forward.

"May I?" Dane nods slowly, his hands finding their way to my hair. *Show time.*

I suck in half his dick at first, getting myself acquainted to this, the most intimate part of Dane. I pull off, holding the base with my hand, then swallow him again. I'm brand new at sucking cock, but I need it to be amazing. I don't want him to remember just how much of a virgin I am, but if the moans up there are any indication, I'm doing at least a decent job.

Knowing I'm making Dane feel good turns me on like I never would've believed. As much as I want to keep going, after a minute, I pull off to breathe properly. "How is that?" I ask, as I shuck off my shirt in three seconds.

"So good," he groans.

"Well alright then. Glad to be of service." I lean in again slowly, this time, taking him in completely. I grab his firm ass and encourage Dane to guide himself more into my mouth. My eyes water at times, but knowing Dane is enjoying being completely inside me is thrilling. At some point, Dane starts to thrust slightly and pulls my head down just a little bit. It's a little uncomfortable, but I'm still enjoying the ride, and feeling Dane pulse in my mouth makes me hard as a brick.

It dawns on me in that moment; Dane Poorweisz is fucking my face. And I kind of love it.

While I'm enjoying sucking him off, I eventually feel his thighs start to quiver. "Landee..." he whimpers, and I know he's on the precipice of ecstasy. Hearing my first name in Dane's strangled, sexy voice lights something inside me, something I've never felt with anyone before. I don't want to dwell on it now, though; I have a job to finish.

Feeling inspired, I grab his ass and pull him tightly into my throat with force, and that's what does it; Dane howls, shooting in my mouth. I swallow it down—years of drinking protein shakes and alcohol taught me that!—and once he's done, I pull off. It's salty, kind of thick, but I'm overwhelmed by how much of Dane that really was. He's my Dane. I want him to be mine. After the amazing sex we just had, I'm sure of it.

Dane hasn't opened his eyes since he came, so I guide him to the bed and he lies down. I lie down next to him, undoing my pants, my own erection springing free. Before I can jerk off to the sight of him, which would have taken me all of five seconds, he abruptly wakes up and pounces on me. I'm startled for a moment, but the next thing I know, his mouth is on my cock and I forget all rational thought. It only takes him four swallows before I'm orgasming as well.

After coming in his mouth sooner than I care to dwell on, I feel Dane lie back down next to me. He's on his side, staring at me, stroking my arm. We stay like that for a few minutes, catching our breaths. Everything about tonight was perfect, and I only hope it was good for him.

Before I can ask him, he whispers, "This was a fantastic date, Landon." All I can do is smile back. Of course he can read my mind.

25: Dane

The sunlight in my bedroom wakes me up and I feel a warm body next to mine. I look down to see Landon, naked, curled up against me, snoring into my chest. Memories of last night come back: the date, the sex, he and I taking turns going to the communal bathroom late at night, then finally stripping off all our clothes to cuddle in bed.

This has to be a dream. The past several weeks, the dates, the mind-blowing sex with the most beautiful guy I've ever seen—all of it has to be a mirage. None of this can be my reality, because that's just not what I was destined for. I was cursed a long time ago with a messed-up eye, and that led to being alienated; in school, kids made fun of me, then later on, guys never wanted to go out with me. I've acted strong all these years, but that loneliness hurt. Now I have this gorgeous and sweet guy who actually treats me like I'm not ugly, and I don't understand it. When is Landon going to hurt me? Pain is all I've known, but he and I seem to be on the road to a loving, solid relationship.

Did I just say *'loving'*? No way…not yet. Right?

"Morning babe." Landon stretches, still curled up next to

me, then reaches up to peck me on the lips. His use of '*babe*' isn't helping with the mini freak-out I'm having.

I push down these conflicting feelings and smile. "Morning you."

He stares at me with dreamy fondness and adoration. Grinning, he reaches up and strokes my left eye.

"Can I ask you something?"

"Shoot."

"You know we're... um...I like you a lot and respect you."

"Uh-huh."

"So you don't have to answer." Oh. Here it comes.

"Okay."

"You're like, so handsome. I still think you're handsome but... How did your eye get like this?" he asks while stroking the side of my face. He sounds so genuine. He's so unlike all of the other guys who have asked me about this. My closest friends at KU have been kind enough to never talk about it, but with Landon, it's different. Despite any alarms going off in my heart, I want to let him in.

"Honestly? It was congenital."

"Born with it?"

"Yeah. Some kids are born with malformed hearts or no intestines, so in the grand scheme, I'm pretty lucky."

"That's true." He lies back, still staring at me, now stroking my arm. When he doesn't continue, I know it's my turn to let it out.

"Still, life wasn't easy. I never got to watch the older 3D movies because you need two eyes and I'm basically a cyclops," I scoff, but Landon looks concerned.

"Shit, I hadn't even thought of that." He rises onto his elbows, the blanket sliding down. "Wait, people never called you that, right?" He looks like he's starting to get mad.

I shrug. "In elementary school. Kids are dumb, you know."

"Fucking assholes," he mutters. I'm touched to see he wants to defend six-year-old me.

"Don't worry about it. It only made me stronger. That's what my parents used to say," I lament, staring up at the ceiling.

"Fuck, Dane."

"Picture day was the worst." The words are surfacing now. I haven't talked about this to anyone but my middle school therapist. "I begged my parents to let me skip it. It was like, the eye patch singled me out, but my regular face was so ugly that—"

"Hey hey, shh..." Landon reaches over to wipe my eyes. I hadn't realized tears were leaking out. "You're not ugly Dane. You're not." He stares at me intently, but I keep looking away. "Don't ever say that about yourself, not in front of me."

I sniff and nod, and he leans in to kiss me again. A warmth spreads down my whole body. Telling him about my past feels like jumping out of a plane, and Landon is the parachute I hope will open up to guide me down.

After a few more minutes of making out in bed, I feel my erection poke him on the hip. "I should go. I have a shit ton of homework to do," Landon mutters against my lips.

"Same."

"But first..." A mischievous grin spread across his face. He pulls off the covers to reveal that he is hard as steel, too. "We should probably take care of these..."

I giggle, raising my eyebrows. "To help us concentrate on our homework."

"Exactly!" Landon chuckles as he lines up his hard cock against mine. He reaches down and grabs us both gently. "It's for academic reasons."

"Of course," I moan, feeling him push against me. I grab his ass and guide him along, the arousal coursing through my skin.

That's how we spend the next few minutes our morning: frotting, rubbing, moaning, and gasping, until finally we both burst all over each other.

26: Dane

The next six weeks fly by. As the spring semester heats up, so does my budding, pseudo-secret relationship with Landon. We manage to keep our hands off each other in dance class despite the knowing glances from Tisha and Val. While not completely a secret, we're not really public either. Sometimes we hang out in his suite to watch movies with his roommates. Other nights we chill and watch TV alone, and it feels wonderfully domestic. Because of his soccer schedule, we go on dates once every other weekend. We get to have lunch semi-regularly during the day, and most nights when he's not 100 percent beat from practice, he sleeps in my room. Sex with him feels better than anything I've done before, and while we haven't graduated to anal yet, I'm constantly satisfied. I guess this is what having an actual boyfriend feels like!

Holy shit I'm in a relationship. *Holy shit, my boyfriend is hot as hell and on the soccer team. Holy shit, I'm dating Landee Landon!*

Most days I expect to wake up and realize this is all just a dream. How else can I explain this gorgeous guy who wants to hang out with me, who makes me a priority? Landon is so thoughtful and fun to be around that he's been making me fall slowly every day for weeks. The other shoe has to drop.

Life finally decides to send me a curveball, but not via the disappointment I'm used to; I receive an email from the RDC Manhattan asking if we could chat. That's gotta be a good sign, right?

I dial the number and get an answer in three rings. "Regal Dance Company, Evelyn speaking."

"Hi! Evelyn, this is Dane Poorweisz."

"Dana, hi! So glad you called! How are you?"

"Good, good." I'm in my room alone, and my leg is shaking in anticipation.

"Pleased to hear it. So I'll get right to it. Dana, we want you for one of the three national slots for Performance Intern. If, of course, you're interested."

"Oh my God, yes!" I'm shouting in my room and I don't even care. I got the position!

"Wow, glad to make you happy!" She laughs. "However we should still go over the logistics. You said you're still a junior at Korham University?"

"Yes, is that a problem?"

"Well, the thing is, initially we spoke of a ten-week summer internship. However, some members of our company have had to step down, so the three national slots will be several months instead."

"Months?"

"Seven months to be exact."

"Can I just do the ten-week option?"

"Unfortunately no." I can hear her wincing over the phone. "We want to cultivate newer dancers to potentially join us full-time. It requires a lot of your time, with teaching tours all over the East Coast. Then, in December, you'll likely be a stage-hand, if not main cast for *The RDC Christmas Picturesque.* Effectively, it's a big commitment. Thus, we're only offering the seven-month contract, from June until early January. You would either need to graduate early or take a one-semester sabbatical from school."

My mind buzzes with conflicting ideas. My dream internship leading to my dream job means being away from KU for at least half a year. I'd be leaving Landon.

"I...I don't think I have enough credits to graduate in a month."

"We realize that's very soon. We apologize if this is inconvenient. I recommend you talk to your faculty about a sabbatical. If you're still interested, that is."

"I am! I'm just...It's a lot to think about." I'm trying not to sound ungrateful. This is a huge deal. People come from all over the world to watch the RDC Manhattan. Celebrities and politicians go out of their way to see *The RDC Christmas Picturesque.* If I take this, I'm almost guaranteed a full-time position after I graduate.

"We understand. It is a big commitment, one that shouldn't be taken lightly." Evelyn goes on about logistics—payment, hours, etc.—for a few more minutes before she says she'll email me the contract.

"We'll need to hear from you within a week."

"Understood."

"Great! We hope you choose to join us Dana. The RDC could use someone as talented as you. Take care, goodnight."

"Thanks. Goodnight Evelyn."

After hanging up, I take a deep breath, then another. I sit down at my desk and boot up my email. I scroll through all the fine print, then read over it again. *"I need to think about my future,*" I tell myself, as I click on all the buttons to sign the contract. New York City, here I come.

27: Landon

Dating Dane has been fantastic these past few weeks. I thought the idea of being in a relationship with a dude would be weird, but it's not. Dane makes me smile and laugh. He understands me, doesn't judge me, and for the first time in my life, I feel like someone is putting me first, the real me. It's indescribable how solid I feel after all these years; being with Dane just feels right.

I keep trying to find a downside to dating him, but I really can't. Screw the homophobes in the world, screw all the judgment I might get. It's all worth it to have this guy by my side.

However, this past week, he's been acting kind of funny. His texts are shorter, and he's blown me off for a couple of lunch dates, saying he has lots of homework. As the semester winds down, it's understandable; our dance showcase is right around the corner. Still, I can't shake the feeling that he's hiding something.

After not getting to hang out for two whole days, I decide to call him.

"Hello?"

"Hey babe," I chirp. "What are you up to now? Busy?"

"Um..."

"Wanna get lunch?"

"Oh crap, I did forget to eat today."

"Sweet. Union food court?"

"Um, I don't know."

"Please? I haven't seen you in like over a day! Pretty please?"

"Uh, okay." He sounds reluctant, but I'll take it!

"See you in ten!" I hang up and go get ready.

I'm anxiously sitting with my food in the corner of the food court. There are a few people around, but no one looking in my direction. As I tap my foot, I spot a familiar red beanie on a gorgeous guy walking toward me. I nearly knock over my drink as I wave frantically, smiling.

"Hey babe!" I greet him as he walks up to the table. I quickly get up and give him a quick peck on the lips. I want much more, but we're in public, and I don't think either of us is ready for public displays of affection.

"Hey yourself," he says and sits down next to me. I wait for him to tell me about his day, but he proceeds to eat his chicken fingers in silence. My eyes dart between him and my food as I eat. It still feels like Dane is hiding something.

"I'll never get over that," I mutter.

"What?"

"Kissing you. I'll never get tired of that."

A blush creeps on his face as he smiles. I put my hand on his knee as we continue to eat. We spend the next five minutes catching up on our last two days. Just talking with him relaxes me.

After some time, I spot two familiar figures walk up to us, trays in hand.

"Hey guys!" Steven says.

"Sup," Ravi adds, smiling and sitting down across from me. "Mind if we join you?"

"Of course not. It's good to see you," Dane says.

"So...how are things?" Steven's voice is laced with innuendo as he points between Dane and me with a fork. I turn to look at my boyfriend to see him stiffen.

"Things are good." he replies.

"Awesome," Ravi says, with a mouth full of food.

"I'm so happy for you two." Steven is grinning at me and I feel my face get hot.

"Uh, Steven! What's new in the art world?" I ask. We spend the next few minutes making small talk about whatever projects Steven has going on.

All too soon, Dane is done, and says, "I gotta meet with an advisor. This was fun, though! I'll talk to you guys later." He stands up, hesitates for a moment, looking at me. I think he wants to kiss me, but his face is torn with conflict. Eventually, he walks away, throwing his trash on his way out.

With Dane gone, I slump back in my chair, frowning.

"What's wrong?" Ravi asks.

I sigh. "I think Dane is pulling away from me."

"Aww, you really like him, huh?" Steven's tone is teasing.

"I do."

"I'm happy for you bro," Ravi says. "But what

makes you think he's pulling away?"

"I don't know. He's been acting weird this week. Like he's too busy for me."

"Don't you have your dance thing next week?"

"Yeah, our showcase."

"He's probably super stressed about that."

"Yeah, he's a TA," Steven adds. "His credits are on the line."

"Yeah, maybe that's it." I nod my head in thought. "I should go, though. I'll see you guys later."

"Later man. Any time you wanna talk, we're here for you," Ravi replies.

I get up to throw out my trash, but not before hearing Steven whisper to Ravi, "Remember when we were going through that?"

28: Dane

I only tell my parents about the internship. I don't want to tell Landon because it will just shock him into realizing the truth: we can't stay together. He'll find someone else while I'm away in the fall, I'm sure of it, so I might as well end things now. *"He was bound to find someone else eventually, someone prettier, fit to be with a gorgeous guy like him. Our relationship was never meant to last,"* I reason in my head.

While I want a clean, amicable break, our big semester show is next week, and I can't risk messing that up for either of us. For now, I'll enjoy being with Landon. Just because I'm leaving doesn't mean I don't have feelings for him and we can't have fun. I care for him deeply, but our lives are headed in different directions. They always were. This was just…a fling, I guess.

Maybe if I say it to myself enough, it will hurt less.

I want to ease away from Landon, perhaps have him sleep over less, but tonight's text message seems heavier than usual. We had lunch with Steven and Ravi three days ago, and I know he had an away game today in the afternoon. Tonight, however, he's asking to sleep over, practically pleading in the text, so how can I say no?

When I open the door, he's got his bag as usual, but his eyes are downcast. Gone is the smile I'm so used to. Shit.

"Hey, baby, what's wrong?"

"Ugh," he moans. He walks in and puts his bag down, then sits on a chair. He puts his elbows on his knees and props his head up, still not looking at me.

I pull up a chair beside him and put my hand on his back. Now that I think about it, I've never actually seen him in bad mood before. He's always got that party boy facade, and when he lets it down around me, he's typically in good spirits. "Landee?"

"I'm so stupid," he mutters.

"What?"

"Ugh...it's dumb. I don't wanna bore you with the details. It's not gonna sounds like a big deal to you."

"What isn't?" I rub his back and he's still not looking at me.

"We lost the game today."

"Oh."

"'Cause of me."

"Huh?"

"It's so stupid but like... I had the ball in the last five minutes, ready to break the tie. I had it, I *had* it but I failed to score."

I'm not sure how to respond, but he seems so dejected. "Oh, I'm sorry babe."

"And because I couldn't finish, the other team was able to get their counter attack going. Eventually, they scored, and we didn't have enough time to come back from it, so they took the win. I can't help but feel partly responsible. Fuck, I was so angry in the locker room."

Wow, he really is heartbroken over this. I rub his back some more and think about my rudimentary understanding of soccer. "Don't be so hard on yourself. You're not the only guy on the team."

"Yeah but I *had* it. Everyone was counting on me to do what I've done like a million times before."

I stand up and get behind him and start to rub his shoulders. He's so tense, I want to take his stress away. "Aw babe. I promise you'll bounce back from this. The whole team will. I bet you'll go into your next game...and like... score a *hundred* goals!"

This earns me an honest chuckle. "Seems unrealistic." I can hear him smiling.

"Okay then, ninety-nine goals. All from you."

"Doubt it, but thanks for your confidence." He laughs, and I feel his shoulders relax. An idea strikes me.

"Hey, why don't you take off your clothes and get on the bed?"

He gives me a puzzled look. "Not that I mind but—"

"I just want to massage your back! No funny business I swear."

Landon gets up and does what he's told. He strips down to his boxers and goes to lie on the mattress, face down. I apply some lotion to my hands and straddle his lower back. While I've never done this, I know what feels good when I've gotten a massage, so I try to follow that memory.

I push up on the muscle around Landon's shoulder blades. He really does have a sexy back—sexy everything, to be honest. As I push back down, I hear him groan and his body relaxes. Landon is so stressed, probably from beating himself up, and it dawns on me: I want to take that stress away. Forget about us possibly breaking up in the near future, I want him to feel better *now*.

After ten minutes of working his back and arm muscles, I hear him moan, "Mmm...thank you, love."

Landon calling me a pet name always gets my stomach to flutter, but I refuse to read into the *L-word*. It's just a nickname. I lean down and kiss his cheek. He starts to get up, so I move to let him turn over. I take a good look at him, half naked on my bed; this never gets old. With the miles of lean muscle coursing over every inch of him, I could plant my mouth on his skin for days.

He is so sexy that I'm overcome with the need to chase this moment. I leap up top and straddle him again, this time whipping off my shirt. He grabs my thighs, and I lean in, kissing him. I moan as my tongue enters his mouth, enjoying the scent I've gotten used to but will never take for granted. It's so 100 percent Landon, and he's 100 percent mine. As I get hard and feel his erection poking me, I realize I want to be 100 percent his.

Feeling my stomach for a moment, I thank the heavens I haven't eaten much today. Good, my preparations should be minimal. I break apart from Landon and whisper, "I want to try something."

Landon nods, lust filling his eyes. I get off and say, "I'm going to the bathroom. I'll be back in five minutes, and I want you naked."

His eyebrows jump but a smile brightens his face. "I thought you said no funny business?"

I lean back in and peck him on the lips. "There's nothing funny about what I want from you tonight, baby."

I dash away, but before I leave the room, I reach into my desk drawer. Deep within the bowels of the clutter, I find what I need and throw it at Landon. His eyebrows jump again, looking at the chain of condoms I've tossed at him. When he looks up at me, I simply wink and walk out the door.

No tomorrow, no yesterday. I need Landon, tonight.

29: Landon

Holy crap, this is happening, this is going to happen, holy crap!

I'm stroking my erection when I see Dane walk back into the room. He looks so sexy shirtless, but I can't lie—I'm nervous. I've had sex before, but those girls never mattered, not the way Dane matters to me. While he might not be ready to hear this, I know for sure that I've been falling in love with him these past few months. When he calls me 'baby,' my insides fizzle just knowing that he's mine.

Right now, though, he's about to make me his. He opens up the packet of lube on the desk. "Do you want to be inside me Landon?" His voice is husky and drenched with hunger. All I can do is nod in response.

He smiles, then straddles me again and kisses me, all the while fingering himself. Fuck, this is so hot. No girl has ever taken charge in bed with me. Forget about those girls. Forget about all other humans or bedrooms in the universe; it's just Dane and me right now.

After kissing some more, he slides the condom on me, then scoots forward. Before I can ask him any more details, he leans over then slowly slides down, taking me in. As he envelopes the first half of my cock, I gasp.

Fuck.

It's so tight, and it feels so good. I'm inside Dane, the most amazing man I've ever known.

"How's that stud?" he whispers, as he begins to rock forward. My entire length is inside him.

"Uhhh...so good," I grunt.

"Yeah?" He begins to touch his own hardness between us, and it sets off something inside me. I grasp his hips firmly and start to match him with my thrusts, picking up speed. "Oh fuck, Landee."

My eyes roll back at hearing my name like that, a prayer on his lips. Sex has never felt anything like this. I'm overwhelmed with sensation and emotion. I need this release. I need him to know I'd do anything for him.

Not even three minutes later, I feel the familiar delicious pressure build. "I love...this..." I grab his ass firmly. I was so close to saying *"You. I love you, Dane."*

"Yeah?" He's still stroking himself.

"Yeah. I'm gonna..."

"Give it to me," he moans.

"Dane, I'm gonna—" That's all I get out before a strangled moan leaves my lips. I close my eyes and see the sun, the moon, Jupiter, and all the other planets. This orgasm is one for the record books. Without even being done, I hear Dane whimper and clench around me. Hot semen splashes onto me, and it fills me with delight knowing that this amazing guy just came while I was inside him.

While I catch my breath, he eases off of me. A minute later, I feel him use some clothes to clean up my chest. At least I think that's what's happening. My eyes are half closed and I'm still lost in the galaxies of post-orgasmic haze. Finally, he crawls into bed and wraps himself around my torso, his head on my shoulder.

Fuck, I'll never forget this night as long as I live. I've had sex before, but screw the past. Dane was my first time. I want him to be all my next times as well.

A week later, I'm waiting at the side of the stage in the Fine Arts building's performance space. I'm wearing a leotard and tight T-shirt, the standard all-black ensemble Ryn told us to wear. I look out into the crowd and see a packed house. I spot Ravi, Steven, Omar, Kareem, and Stacia, all sitting together. I'm touched they all came out. I guess they were serious when they claimed they wanted to support me.

"Hey, we should probably hang back." I turn around to see Dane. His musculature looks so defined in his leotard. I hope I don't get a boner on stage, but I'm too nervous to, anyway. "We'll be up soon, and the audience shouldn't see us here."

I move further back and lean on a nearby wall. I drill and drill the choreography in my head, hoping I don't trip Val or make a fool of myself in any way. It isn't even about me looking idiotic in front of my friends; it's about making Tisha, Val, and Professor Ryn look good by association. And of course, Dane. I need to be amazing for the man I've fallen in love with.

Five months ago, if you'd told me I'd be racking my brain on stage before a dance recital so I could prove myself worthy of the man I love, I'd probably have kicked you in the nuts.

"Hey." Dane's hand touches mine and my eyes bolt open. "You alright?"

"Yeah…" I nod once, then again more aggressively before looking up. "Yeah, totally, I'm fine, I'm…I'm fine."

"You don't need to be nervous. You've done amazing all semester. Just being here, you're definitely passing the class. You'll probably get an A, to be honest."

"Yeah but…I don't wanna disappoint—"

"Your friends?"

"You." His eyebrows jump, and I bite my lip. I look down at my hands and notice they're shaking. *Fuck, what has this guy done to me?* "So I gotta just, do better, *be* better and I —"

Dane cuts me off by putting his lips on mine, holding the kiss hard. When we finally part, it's my turn to look shocked. We've never kissed during a dance rehearsal, so this is just crazy!

"Seriously?!" Val whispers angrily. I turn to see the girls; Tisha looks unimpressed, shaking her head, whereas Val straight up looks like she wants to punch me. "We finally get to see this *now*?! Right before we perform for everyone?!"

"You knew?" I whisper right back.

"Honey, everyone knows. The whales in the ocean probably know," Tisha says with a grin. "We're just mad because Dane won't give us any details."

"And you drop this"—Val points at my lip then points at Dane—"Right before we're going on stage?"

I turn to see Dane trying to hold back a laugh, his face a shade darker. "Uh, sorry?" I shrug at the girls. They roll their eyes and move forward in line as the first group goes on stage.

As soon as the first few notes of the song hit, I feel my muscle memory kick into overdrive. It's a similar feeling to being on the field for an important match, yet very different. My goal isn't to win or get the ball. My goal is to remember everything Dane taught me. I need to feel my way through this. I muster the confidence I usually bring to the field and tune out all other thoughts. Right now, it's me, the stage, the music, and the moves. Five, six, seven, AND...

We absolutely kill it on stage for our four-person routine. I hit all the moves with precision and in time. I know this because if I hadn't, Val would have tripped. She's dynamite in my arms when we do the Latin couples portion; she invokes the stage presence I've gotten used to seeing, but times a hundred. I don't focus on Tisha and Dane, but they're the stronger couple, so I have no doubt they hit their moves correctly. As the final act of the show, the entire class comes together and we do a group modern-ballet fusion. I'm proud to say I don't trip over myself once.

After the show, we're in the lobby chatting with various audience members who are congratulating us. It's mostly parents with some friends and faculty floating about. I chat briefly with my boys before they bid me good night and I walk over to Dane. He's talking with Tisha, Jonathan, Val, and Dominic—him again?—when an older couple approaches.

"Bravo! No, brava! You were all wonderful!" The older woman gives Dane a big old kiss on the cheek.

"Thanks Mom."

149

"Great job, all of you!" the stout man with her says, putting a hand on Dane's shoulder.

Dane turns to the rest of us. "Guys these are my parents. Mom, Dad, this is…the group!"

"Hi *the group!*" Dane's dad cheerfully greets us.

"We wanna thank you all so much for being such a tight-knit dance ensemble for our Dana!" his mom says. "In fact, we wanted to invite you all to come over for a picnic at the house tomorrow to celebrate! There's so much to be thankful for."

"It's my birthday on Monday!" Dane blurts. "And it's also to celebrate our semester showcase!" Huh. He sounds rather defensive. Almost like he really is hiding something…

"So how about it?" Dane's dad asks.

"Can I bring my boyfriend?" Tisha asks, holding on to Jonathan.

"Of course! You kids can bring dates!" Dane's mom exclaims.

"I guess I'm taking this guy!" Val laughs, getting on her toes to pat Dominic on the head. He smiles and nods as she does so.

"How about you, young man?" Dane's dad looks at me and I freeze up.

"Uhh…" I don't know how much Dane has told them about us. Shit. I look at Dane who's looking similarly concerned. In fact, the entire group looks scared, as if I'm about to set off a bomb. "Nope. Just me!"

"Well alright!" We all chuckle a breath of relief. "Hey I hope you kids like potato salad!"

"What's not to like?!" Dominic laughs, and everyone starts to chat as Dane hugs his parents goodbye.

30: Landon

"Are you sure this is okay?" I'm driving to Dane's house while adjusting the collar of my plaid, short-sleeved button-down shirt. "I don't want it to seem too casual, like I don't take anything seriously."

"It looks fine," Dane assures me. "It's just a friendly afternoon picnic. You can relax. My parents won't bite." He puts his hand on my bare elbow and I feel my anxiety dissipate. I send a smile his way, and his eye sparkles.

"Gag me," Dominic mutters in the backseat. He had been silent for the past twenty minutes, so I completely forgot Dane offered to give him a ride. I roll my eyes while Dane bites his lip to hold back a laugh. While I've come to realize he's not interested in my boyfriend, I'm only now starting to warm up to the idea of him as a friend. "You guys are cute but gross."

"Sorry man, I'll be sure to keep my hands off Landon during the party." He grabs my arm again and throws me a look that makes my insides do a backflip. We've been dating for weeks, and he still has this effect on me.

"Speaking of which, do your parents know about you two?"

I shoot Dane a look, and his mouth opens, then closes. "Umm..."

"Got it," Dominic chirps while fiddling with his phone. "I won't say a word. But you two are pretty obvious. You might want to stay away from each other. And not look at each other. At all."

I can hear his smirk while I grip the wheel tighter. I forgot to have this conversation with Dane, and I sure as hell don't want to while Dominic is here. We both agreed on being discreet, but I still want to impress Dane's family. I don't think he realizes how much I've fallen for him and that I want a future with him.

The Poorweisz house is only about forty minutes away from KU. It's this tiny suburban home, but there's a massive backyard; that's where we find ourselves on this warm and sunny spring afternoon. Walking in, I notice a giant tree with a tire swing dangling from it, along with some lawn games on the grass. Tisha, Val, and Jonathan are already there when we arrive, sitting at the large picnic table with cups in hand. Dane's dad is starting the grill while his mom is sitting down chatting with the girls.

The food isn't ready yet, so Dane's mom insists we go and hang out. We play two rounds of a game where we pair up to throw discs into a can and see which team can score the most points. Dominic and I are on a team because apparently I'm "too athletic" and need to help someone who's as uncoordinated as him—his words, not mine—while Jonathan and Dane take the other side. The girls watch us and play with a Hacky Sack. Everyone seems to be having a good time.

After a few rounds, Dane's mom calls him over to ask him to help set up something, and I take this as a good opportunity to show that I can be helpful in this family. I follow Dane, while the others go to take pictures on the tire swing.

"I need help with the watermelon, honey," Dane's mom says. She turns to me next. "We got this, you stay."

Before I can object, I hear Mr. Poorweisz holler, "Yeah, I could use some help by the grill!" I give Dane a pleading look. He looks at me and shrugs slightly as he walks inside; I interpret his look as him saying, '*It'll be fine!*'

I approach Mr. Poorweisz and notice the food is all neatly placed on the already burning grill. "So you're Mr. Landon, correct?" He has a hefty voice and a large mustache that shakes when he talks. Dane really looks more like his mom.

"Uh yes...Mr. Poorweisz, sir." Why are my hands trembling? "Do you need assistance?"

"So polite! I don't need help. I just wanted to see how you were doing."

"I'm fine!" I squeak, my voice coming out higher than usual. He continues to push the meat on the grill around, glancing at me intermittently.

"Dana was so grateful when you drove him to New York City that weekend."

"It was nothing." I shrug.

"Nonsense, it meant a lot to him! And to us. You really came through for him." He pauses to look directly at me, studying me. My heart starts to beat faster, like I'm being interrogated. "You're a... true friend."

"No problem, sir. Dane is a good friend of mine."

"He doesn't talk about his...*friends* too much." He raises his eyebrows like he's trying to signal something. *Oh shit.* "I just hope you're treating him right."

"Uh...I'd like to think so!" I'm twiddling my thumbs, desperately hoping for a big old bird to swoop down and pluck me from this conversation.

"Uh-huh." He scrutinizes my face again, all while pushing the meat around. "He cares about you a lot. I hope you know that."

My shoulders relax a little, and I lower my voice. "I care about him too."

"Are you two using protection? Because safe sex is—"

"Dad!" We both turn to see Dane, his face etched with horror. He's holding a massive tray of sliced watermelon a few yards away from us.

"What?" Dane's dad whines.

"Um...*the potato salad is ready!*" Dane shouts, and the others join us at the table.

I give a polite nod to Mr. Poorweisz as I slip away, but not before seeing his knowing grin.

Dane sets up bread and chips while his mom passes around plates. I'm seated at the corner of the table as far away from Dane as possible. Dominic might have a point —if I'm farther away from him, I'll be less likely to brush his hand or lean in for a kiss. While it's obvious his dad knows something, Dane and I still want to be discreet.

Mr. Poorweisz hands out some meats from the grill while Dane helps pour out soda for everyone. Before I can start eating, however, Mr. Poorweisz stands at the end of the table and claps his hands.

"I would like to say a few words before we eat. Dane, I'm so proud of you."

"Aw, Dad." Dane is rolling his eyes but smiling. They really are a cute family. It warms my heart to see parents who put together all this just for their son. While my parents have given me a lot, they've never once come to my college games or even inquired about my friends. I'm a little jealous to see what I've been missing, but I hope maybe one day the Poorweisz family can accept me into their lives in a similar way.

"I was proud of all you kids on stage yesterday! You all were fantastic! And son, I hope you have a blessed birthday on Monday and continue to perform your best this summer, this fall, and at the New York Christmas show!"

Huh? Why is he referring to *The Christmas Picturesque*? It's not like Dane got the internship. Because if he did, he would have told me...

Dane's mom stands and holds up a plastic cup. "Let's all raise a toast!" Everyone lifts their drinks.

"To good friends...and to the art of dance!" Mrs. Poorweisz announces.

"And to Dane getting the seven-month internship at the RDC Manhattan!" Mr. Poorweisz adds.

"Oh, of course! Congrats on that! Cheers!" Mrs. Poorweisz taps cups with Tisha while Dominic touches my cup.

I think everyone at the table is murmuring and congratulating Dane. I'm not sure, I can't hear anyone over the buzzing noise in my ear. I look over to my boyfriend. He laughs at something Val says, but before he can turn to me, he looks down quickly at his food. He's pointedly avoiding my gaze, and all of a sudden I have no appetite.

Dane got a seven-month RDC internship? And he didn't tell me?

31: Dane

The car ride home is tense. We mostly just listen to the radio and I occasionally small talk with Dominic in the back seat about whatever song is playing. Landon's knuckles are nearly white as he grips the steering wheel, paying close attention to the road.

When we get to campus, we drop Dominic off near the student union because he had to pick up some stuff at the QPU room. After he gets out, Landon still isn't looking at me.

"Do you want me to drop you off near your dorm?" he asks, his tone even.

"I'd rather wait for you to park," I reply quietly. This reminds of the first night we kissed when I said something similar. He and I have come a long way in the past several weeks.

Once he finally pulls into a spot and shuts off the car, he undoes his seatbelt and looks down at the steering wheel. Shit, I don't like Landon being this upset at me.

I undo my seatbelt and look down as well. "I'm

sorry. The internship goes from mid-June to mid-January. So I'll need to take a sabbatical from KU for a semester."

I play with my thumbs for a bit. After a weighted minute of silence, I can't take it anymore, so I say, "Look, the RDC Manhattan is like the biggest opportunity for a new performing artist."

Landon finally looks at me. He looks so tired and hurt. "I know. I'm happy for you."

"You are?"

"I want you to succeed. You deserve everything. You're like the best dancer I know."

He sounds so defeated that I abstain from pointing out I'm one of the only dancers he knows. "Are you mad?" I whisper.

"Why didn't you tell me?" he croaks. "We tell each other everything. This is like a life-changing opportunity."

"That's just it. It's life-changing. Landon, I didn't want things to change between us."

"So what? You were just going to leave KU for months and not tell me?"

"I was gonna tell you after finals. That way, we can enjoy the time we still have left together."

Landon looks like I just insulted his mother. "What's that supposed to mean? I'm not leaving you."

"But I'm leaving *you*!" I sigh and rub my temple.

"It's only for a semester." I look up and see a hopeful shrug. "I'll wait for you."

"Really?"

He bites his lip and looks down. Then, he turns and leans to grab something in the backseat pocket.

"I wanna give you this now instead of Monday,"

he grunts, his body still twisted.

"Oh?"

When he sits back down, he's holding a tiny red-and-yellow box. The gift wrap is all mangled, so I can tell Landon worked really hard to package this.

"What is this?"

"It's your birthday present. Open it."

I carefully take the gift and insert my finger into one of the malformed flaps of paper. Tearing it away slowly, I reveal the glossy cover of a book. It reads *101 Free Things to do in Manhattan*, and my heart just about melts.

"I um...believed you'd get the internship. But even if you didn't, I figured you'd come visit me, maybe?"

I look up to see a cautious but hopeful smile. I really don't deserve this man.

"Landon, this is so sweet. I'm gonna cherish this, thank you...but the internship isn't just New York City. I'll be doing workshop tours every other week along the East Coast. I'd be leaving you, like a lot."

He shrugs in response. "I'll still wait for you."

"Seriously?" *Just pull back Landee. Find someone who's as beautiful and worthy as you, please.*

"Yeah." He takes his hand and places it on mine. "Of course."

Before the alarm bells can go off, I lean in and kiss him. His lips part, and his left hand finds its way through my hair. We kiss and moan, tongues tasting the other person.

We part for a moment and Landon says, "I won't leave you. You're my boyfriend and I..." I can tell he wants to say something, something I refuse to guess, but he holds back. "I'm crazy for you."

We lean in and kiss again. "Same," I moan in between kisses. I know I need to cut things off, but fuck, I'm addicted to the way he tastes. "Crazy...mm...So crazy."

"Your dad totally knows about us," he giggles against my lips.

"Please don't talk about my dad if you ever want me to get hard again," I mutter while kissing him. We both break apart in a fit of laughter.

Once we calm down, I stroke his cheek and look at him. He is so handsome. How am I going to say goodbye to him?

"Are we cool?" I ask, my voice softer than usual.

"We're better than cool. We're both crazy for each other."

The next four weeks are filled with hustling as our junior year ends. I submit the paperwork for my one-semester sabbatical—Professor Ryn is so thrilled that I got the internship. Everyone on campus is buzzing after finals with end-of-the-year parties and packing up our dorms. I spend the week between school ending and the start of the internship at my parents' house. I phone chat with Landon every night, but it sucks not having him in my arms.

Today I'm in Queens unpacking my suitcase in my Aunt Cindy's house. The commute to the studio will require two trains and will take almost an hour each way, but it's so worth it. Landon suggested I stay in his house, but there's no way I can accept living in that mansion. My aunt works a lot and was gracious enough to give me as much space as I need, but I'll be touring for several weeks anyway, so I have to get used to living on the road.

I sit on the bed in the guest room and take a deep

breath, looking around. It's all happening. My dream of being a professional performing artist starts tomorrow. Thinking of my future, my first thought is of Landee. I miss him, but I need to get used to missing him. I've been trying to will myself to take a step back from our relationship, but over the phone just doesn't feel right. In fact, none of it feels right, but I need to make a choice for the next several months. The logical decision is to cut ties with him for now, but I can't find the words to tell him.

I scroll through pictures of us on my phone. There's one photo from the end-of-semester fair on campus, and he's holding me while I take a selfie. The sun is shining on us, but his smile is brighter than any star. How am I going to let him down?

My phone buzzes and his face appears. I press the button to accept Landon's call.

"Hello?"

"Hey babe!" he chirps. "You all settled in?"

"Just about. How are you?"

"Bored at home. Listen, I know we agreed you have to focus on the internship, and tomorrow is your first day, but I was thinking..."

"Thinking what?"

"Wanna stay over?"

"What?!"

"It's just for one night!" he blurts defensively. "And think about it, you'll be like a lot closer to the studio. Hell, you can even walk if it's nice out."

"Landon..."

"You can take the guest bedroom! No funny business, I swear. My parents already said it's okay. They think you're sweet. Anyway, they're gone for business half the time, so it's just me, the twins, and the housekeeper."

I sigh. He does have a point. It's closer and would be easier.

"Please. Pretty please, Dane. I miss you."

I bite my lip. "Just one night?"

"Absolutely. Afterward you'll be back in Queens."

"Well, you drive a hard bargain Landee."

"I have been told I'm charming." I can hear his smirk through the phone.

"I'll pack my bag."

"Yes," he whispers. He clears his throat. "I mean uh...bet! I will...see you soon."

I roll my eyes and hang up. What is this boy doing to me?

32: Dane

That night I have dinner with Landon, Link, Kara, and their live-in housekeeper, Marta. We order in from a Jamaican restaurant, and it's very relaxing getting to know everyone. I keep trying to ignore the gnawing feeling that I'm betraying my plans to step back from our relationship. I need to focus on my future as a performing artist.

My boyfriend gives me one chaste goodnight kiss before we call it a night. It's *so* tempting to sleep in his bedroom, but I need to focus on this internship, not Landee. He agreed on no funny business so I can get some good rest, so, instead, I take the guest room next to his like last time. As I lie in the darkness, I look over at my phone. It's almost eleven, I really should go to sleep since tomorrow is my big day. The stakes are high. My rest is important, but my mind is buzzing. I'm missing Landon even though he's only one door away.

My lack of sleep is further proof that I shouldn't be with him anymore. That logic is overridden by another thought: maybe just one more goodnight kiss wouldn't hurt, right? I get up and open the bedroom door, only to see

Landon standing there already, hand up in a knocking position. The hallway is dark, but I can still see him in his tank top and pajama pants. It's so silent. For a moment, all I can hear is him breathing softly.

Before I can say anything, he grabs my face and kisses me, hard. There's nothing relaxing about this; his mouth is aggressive, and my lips and tongue are along for the ride. I moan into him and take three steps back, and Landon follows me. Pretty soon, I fall back onto the bed and he straddles me. We kiss and kiss, our cocks aching against each other.

Another dark moment passes by and our clothes are on the floor. He kisses my neck, and I bite my lip trying not to make any noise. I gasp as he moves his mouth down, sucking on each nipple, then trailing kisses down my abs. We're both on fire, and I never want it to stop. The logical part of me that told me to pull back is out for the night.

I pull Landon back up, and he's just as breathless as I am as he kisses my neck again. We haven't spoken yet, our hormones guiding us. I let the hunger take me as I line up our hard cocks. Landon whimpers, holding still for a moment, then he begins to thrust. The friction feels so good I'm seeing stars. I gasp into his face as he takes me closer to ecstasy. I grip us both harder, and a few thrusts later, I feel him shoot. I catch his mouth with mine, and that's all it takes to send me over the edge. Fireworks go off behind my eyelids as I hiss the word *"fuccckk"* and shoot all over the both of us.

Entwined in a sticky mess, we both immediately drift off.

That was the best sleep I've had in two weeks. I

wake up to sunlight streaming into the Landon guest bedroom. I turn over to see my boyfriend lying there, still slumbering. He looks so gorgeous that I bask in the enjoyment of just looking at him. Stretching, I turn over to grab my phone, noticing how light it is for 7 a.m. I look at the display: *8:45 a.m.*

What.

Shit.

My first day starts *in fifteen minutes*. I bolt out of bed and immediately scroll through my phone, trying to see if there's a glitch, but no, it's definitely way past my wake-up time. Fuck! I scramble to the bathroom in just my briefs and try to pee and brush my teeth at the same time—a difficult feat to do even when you're not panicking.

When I get back into the room, I haphazardly grab my clothes and shove them into a bag. "Shit... shit." I murmur. I'm gonna be late for my first day.

"What's up?" Landon groans, wiping his eyes.

"I'm fucking late," I hiss. "It's almost nine."

"Seriously?" He bolts uprights, still naked.

"Yes!" I bark with fury. I'm looking down but I'm still hopping in an effort to get my pants on faster. "Shit, I knew this was a mistake."

"It'll be alright babe."

"No, no, it won't. Being late on the first day? That's gonna look terrible. I must have forgotten to turn my alarm on when I was hooking up with you. I feel like an idiot."

"Well now, last night wasn't *that* bad," he says, trying to lighten the mood.

I'm still freaking out as I pat my pockets to make sure I have my keys, wallet, and phone. "Yes it was. I gotta go."

"Well let me walk you out." He quickly gets up and puts on his underwear.

"No, you've done enough, thank you." I sound bitter and rude, but really I'm just in a mad rush. "I know the way out."

"Uh okay? Bye, I guess." He sounds irritated but I don't care. I can't risk thinking about his feelings right now. I have to go catch a train. I run down the stairs, not even bothering to say goodbye to anyone who might be in the kitchen. As I close the house gate, I pray to the heavens that the subway is working smoothly and that everyone stays out of my way as I jog down the sidewalk.

--

I finally make it to the stage area inside the RDC Manhattan building and power walk down the aisle. It looks like everyone on stage is still stretching while Evelyn talks to them. Looking at my phone, I see I'm only about thirty-five minutes late, so hopefully my frantic rush wasn't in vain.

Evelyn spots me dashing up the stairs. "Hey, Dana!"

"Hey!" I wave at everyone as I try to catch my breath and look presentable. Everyone looks up and some people wave. There's about twenty people here of all sorts of ages, ethnicities, and body types—gotta love New York!

"Hey, we were worried about you."

"I'm sorry," I apologize as I sit on the ground near Evelyn.

"Let me guess, subway troubles?" I nod quickly, hoping this is the correct answer. "The subway sucks most of the time. Don't worry about it."

"Yeah, but I'm...I should've caught an earlier one, but—"

"Don't sweat it!" Evelyn turns to the rest of the group. "Raise your hand if the New York City subway has ever made you late for something when you otherwise would have been on time." Everyone raises their hands and I hear some fits of laughter. "See? No big deal. It's your first day. We give lots of leeway."

I breathe a sigh of relief as I sit and stretch, my heels touching and knees out. "That's good to hear."

She turns back to everyone and continues, "So as I was saying, *The RDC Christmas Picturesque* goes back to the early 1920's, when President..." I shake my head and try to focus on her history of dance lecture, but I'm too shaken up by being late.

I can't help but feel like this is exactly what I was afraid of. My relationship with Landon is getting in the way of my potential career as a performer.

That evening, I'm watching the summer sun set over the street in front of my aunt's porch. While I sit out here, knees all bunched up, I'm scrolling through the half a dozen or so texts from Landon. They range from *"Sorry if I made you late."* to *"You got this babe!"* but I haven't replied to any of them. I take a deep breath and hit "dial".

"Hey babe!" He sounds so cheerful, and he picked up on the first ring, which is telling. "How was your first day?"

"It was...good." I press my fingers to my eyes

"Okay, did you get in trouble? For being late?"

"No, actually they were really cool with it."

"Oh that's great!"

168

"Yeah, only because it was the first day. Tomorrow or next week I probably won't be so lucky."

"Well, you're not going to be late again. You learned your lesson and so did I. I will set my own alarm as well whenever you stay over!" He sounds so supportive it hurts my chest. I can't keep letting myself believe that I can be cared for by someone as amazing as him.

"I'm not staying over again." I take a deep breath and sigh. "Landon I don't think we should do this anymore."

"Do what?" he whispers.

"Do this...us...our relationship. We should just call this off. With this internship, I'm gonna be too busy to—"

"No."

"What?"

"Dane, I'm calling a cab, and I'm coming over. You...you are *not* doing this to me over the phone." He sounds all sorts of upset, like he's on the verge of another panic attack. I can't say I blame him, but I'm not sure how to react.

"Landon, it's kind of far, and a cab will cost a lot of money."

"I don't care. If you're gonna do this to me, you'll...you'll have the decency to say it to my face."

I clench my eyes to bite back the tears that threaten to fall. "Landee, please don't make this harder than it has to be."

"Too bad. I'm coming over. I already called the cab to your aunt's place. If you want to tell me to fuck off when I get there, that's fine. But you're doing it to my face."

"Landee—"

"Can't talk now. The cab's here. See you soon, bye!" He rushes out the words before the line goes dead. I toy with my phone in my hands while I wipe my eyes.

It's almost dark by the time Landon texts me that he's here. I walk out the door and close it behind me, not wanting my aunt to hear the shouting match that's about to unfold. I walk down the porch steps as he steps through the gate. He looks concerned but not angry. I'm trying to hold in my sadness, but I'm sure I look more tired than usual.

"Dane."

"Landon, it's for the best." I can't even look at his eyes knowing I'll break.

"Dane, look at me." He lifts my face with his hands and looks right at me. Tears are once again stinging my eyes.

"Landon I don't...I don't want to be with you anymore—" He cuts off my lie with a soft kiss.

"You need to hear some things before you continue." His breath is warm against my lips as he puts his forehead on mine. "First of all, I'm sorry if I made you late or if you think I'm getting in the way of your internship."

"It's not that, Landon—"

"Second, I love you, Dane Poorweisz." I bolt upright. I could not have heard that right. "You heard me. I love you. You stole my heart weeks ago, and I'm not taking it back."

"Landee..."

"I love you, but I never told you 'cause I never thought you felt the same way, and that's fine. You don't have to say it back. It doesn't change what we've had for the past few months. I still love you, but I know you wanna break up."

I sniff and wipe both my eyes, looking down. "I

care about you so much," I whisper. I love him, but he'll never move on and find someone worthy if he knows that. He takes me in his arms and holds me. "But my life... I can't be your boyfriend right now. I'm leaving on tour starting next week and every other week. You deserve someone who's just as beautiful as you, someone still at KU who has their feet on solid ground."

"No one's more beautiful than you." He wipes a tear from my bad eye, and I feel a pain right in my chest. "Shit, Dane, you *are* my solid ground."

"If I don't end things now, you'll be so busy with the soccer season and I'll be here in the fall. I can't have you waiting around for texts from me and... and—"

"Shh." He rubs my back. "I kind of saw this coming. Doesn't mean I'm happy about it, but I get it. I respect your decision."

"Really?" I look back up at him; he's smiling but his eyes are watery. At least, I think they are. I can barely see through my tears. *Why is he not just yelling at me?*

"Yup." He kisses my temple and pulls out his phone. "There. I ordered another cab. It'll be here soon." His voice sounds hoarse and it's filled with so much finality. "I won't bother you for as long you have the internship."

I grab him and bury my face in his neck, breathing him in. "Goodbye, Landee," I whisper. It takes all of my strength to let him go and step back.

As he walks backward to the gate he smiles again. "Not goodbye. This is just a temporary break. I'll see you in the spring semester. Once you're back at KU, I'll try every day to convince you to give us another shot."

I slowly shake my head, tears in my eyes. "You shouldn't wait for me. Please don't, Landon. Just find someone better."

He turns to open the gate and closes it, looking at me again. "Not possible. My heart belongs to you, remember? No take-backs, Dane!" He throws me a charming smile despite the tears in his eyes and I can't help but grin a little.

Soon enough, a car appears and Landon gets in. I watch in the darkness as the cab takes away the only man I've ever loved and the only one who's ever loved me in return.

33: Landon

With my headphones in, I repeatedly press the red upward arrow on the treadmill I'm on. I ramp up the speed until I'm pushed to my limit. My thighs are burning with lactic acid as I jog. After all, this is my fourth two-hour cardio session this week. This, on top of all of our team practices and fall semester games, is straining my body, which is exactly what I want.

The past four months haven't been easy. I spent most of my summer at home, bored with my family. We went to various beaches in the south for two weeks as we do every year, but for obvious reasons, I wasn't having much fun. I drove to visit Omar one weekend, but otherwise, I just spent most of my days jogging around New York.

In August, I returned to campus early for soccer training. I'm living in a campus apartment with Ravi, Steven, and Steven's younger brother, Sly. He just transferred to KU and is a year younger than us. I still hang out with Kareem and Omar regularly. Between my senior year and the fall semester being hugely important for soccer, I've been keeping busy. When I'm not at class or practice, I'm here in the Athletics Center gym enduring whatever exercise I can think of. I try to be in the apartment as infrequently as possible; it's not just the "third-wheel" feeling I get from Ravi and Steven that bothers me anymore. It's that every time I sit still or try to sleep, the pain sets in.

I miss Dane so much.

So I keep busy, sweating my ass off exercising even when I don't have to. I'm grunting and gasping for air as I continue my stride, but before I can crank the speed, I feel the treadmill slow down. Confused, I look down and see a hand is turning off the machine. As I catch my breath, I turn to my right to see Logan staring at me with concern.

I take off my headphones. "What's up, Logan?"

"Landon, what are you doing here?" He sounds equal parts irritated and concerned.

"I'm just jogging," I huff, getting off the machine. "Gotta stay in shape."

"You had practice today, and yet you're jogging again now? You're here almost every night." He motions toward a bench. "Come on. Have a seat."

I don't want to argue with Logan, so I sit down. My muscles hurt at first, not being used to resting, but then my body relaxes. I hunch over, elbows on my knees, and beads of sweat fall down in front of me.

Logan sits next to me. "Tell me what's going on." He sounds stern but nonjudgmental. No one else is around, so I feel at ease to open up to him.

"I just need to keep busy."

"By burning yourself out here? Why don't you go have fun or party or something?"

"Don't feel like it. None of that appeals to me

anymore."

"You still miss him, huh?" I nod at the floor. "I've been there. Not too long ago, actually." I hear him get up, and a moment later he returns with a plastic cup of water. I take it and drink it all, then crumple the cup.

When it's clear I don't want to talk anymore, Logan continues, "You boys are doing really well this season."

I nod. "Yup. We might even make it to finals. Hell, we might even get to be regional champs."

"That's something to be proud of. Look, I've been really low in the past, stuck in shitty situations I can't change. I've found that looking forward to something, anything at all, makes life that much more bearable."

I look up and see Logan gazing out at nothing at all. He may actually be the wisest person I know. In retrospect, he seems a lot happier and more genuine this semester. Must be from his recent relationship. "You might be onto something," I mutter.

"I want you guys to bring home that trophy for the school, but you can't do that by burning yourself out every night. You can't play if you're injured or tired."

"Yeah, you're right."

He pats me on the back. "Go out and have fun. Ravi and the others are going to a party tomorrow. That's something you kids enjoy, right?"

"How'd you know about the party?" I smile as he gets up.

He grins at me. "This building is my baby. I have eyes and ears everywhere, Landee." He points at his eyes and points outward with two fingers.

I chuckle at him as he walks away. I get up and

wipe my face on my shirt, resolving to try and have fun this weekend.

The following evening, I open the door of Steven's car and breathe in the cool October air. Omar, Ravi, Steven, and Sly get out as well and walk past me to the frat house down the block. A year ago, a party like this would have been my scene, but after turning over that new leaf in January, they kind of lost their luster. This was, of course, not because of my resolution to be a better person, but because I found an amazing boyfriend whom I wanted to spend all of my time with.

As I enter the frat house, my nose is assaulted with the familiar smell of cheap beer. Omar goes to mingle, and the rest of us make our way to the kitchen, where a keg is being tapped. I try to plaster on my best fake smile as girls walk past and greet us, no doubt excited to be in the presence of the soccer seniors. Most of us aren't into girls right now anyway. Sly might be queer? I really don't have an eye for these sorts of things.

After filling a cup, I slip away to the upstairs area, already looking for some fresh air. I pass a bunch of guys whispering into girls' ears, no doubt trying to hook up. It's amazing how one year ago, I was just like them, doing whatever it took to get laid, not caring about having a real connection. *Fuck, is there anything I can do to forget about Dane?* Walking through a bedroom with some coats on a bed, I find a door to a small wooden balcony. Finally, some peace and quiet.

I lean on the rail and sip my watered-down beer. The thumping of the music is actually kind of soothing from so far away. I spend the next ten minutes or so idly people-watching and otherwise zoning out.

"Hey." I turn to see Sly walking up to me, cup in hand. He looks so much like his brother, but in the dark, it's obvious where the differences are. He looks tense, like he's hiding something, whereas Steven looks relaxed.

"Hey," I mutter, turning back down to stare at nothing in particular.

"Not in the mood to dance with girls? Or guys? Or whoever you want?"

I shake my head. "Nah, man. I'm kind of a wet blanket nowadays. You?"

"No. Frat parties aren't my scene."

"Then why'd you come?"

"You have one guess."

"Steven wants you to loosen up."

"Bingo. Or rather, for you soccer guys: 'Goalll!'..." He shakes his head and pretends to be a screaming crowd, and that earns him a chuckle out of me. I swivel my cup in my hand as my smile fades away. "Wanna talk about it?"

"About what?"

"About why you're a 'wet blanket.' Steven told me you used to be a party animal."

"That's the old me. Omar does all the partying nowadays. Kareem and Ravi are locked down, and I'm..." I look up to see him staring at me in concern. "I'm not the same guy."

"Ravi mentioned you went through a bad break-up."

"Yup."

"That sucks, man." We both sip our beers and

look out into the night sky.

"Aren't you gonna tell me to get over it? That there's plenty of fish in the sea?"

"Have people told you that?"

"Yup." I take a sip and remember Dane crying as I left his aunt's place on that summer night. "In fact, the guy I can't get over basically told me to move on, to find someone better."

"Huh."

"What?" I raise an eyebrow.

"If you listened to him and you actually *did* find someone else, I'd bet it would hurt him."

"But that's what he wanted me to do. Why would he *want* me to hurt him?"

"Maybe that's all he understands?" I stare at him, perplexed. "We're not all as carefree and accepting of love as my brother. Hell, it even took him a bit to accept Ravi's love, and according to their friend Simone, they had it bad for each other for a while." We both grin at that. "All I'm saying is it can be hard accepting what you don't know."

"And pain...is all he knows." I'm looking down at my cup. Shit, that would explain a *lot* about Dane. If this is true, then I need Dane to realize I would never hurt him.

Sly shrugs, takes a big sip, and looks off in the distance. "This beer is awful. I'm going downstairs to get some more. You wanna come?"

I smile and follow him. "You're the smart brother, aren't you?"

"Most definitely," he replies without hesitation.

We eventually make it downstairs and refill our cups. A few minutes later, we find the others and I actually manage to engage in conversation and laugh for the rest of the night. It's the closest thing to relaxed I've felt in months.

34: Dane

I open the door to my hotel room and toss my duffel into the closet. After three months of being on the road every other week, I've gotten the hang of living out of my bag. Before the door closes, my roommate walks in.

"We crushed it today!" Jung announces. "Nothing like teaching the youth. Those high school kids are gonna make great dancers one day, mark my words."

I met Jung early on in the internship. He got one of the three positions, but he was based in New York City. Like me, he was taking a sabbatical from his senior year of college to pursue this huge opportunity. Because we were the new guys on the block and about the same age, we gravitated toward each other. It was also pretty evident he was gay and a huge dance nerd as well, so we had a lot in common.

"Living the dream," I remark, sitting on my bed and texting my parents.

I really am living a dream though. Being part of the RDC Manhattan means getting paid to learn complicated dance routines, learn the ins and outs of the New York City performing arts scene, as well as touring to give workshops hours away. This week, several of us were tasked with teaching teenagers here in Philadelphia, and we had a blast. Every day I'm learning so much, making professional connections, and solidifying a career I thought was a pipe dream.

While professionally I'm happy and always put on a smile, my home life is a different story. I spend extra time in the studio after work and come home late most evenings just so I can crash as quickly as possible. On my days off, I help my Aunt Cindy with errands or chores—her basement is now spotless because of me. I do anything to keep busy because the moment I stop, the loneliness sets in.

There is no denying it: I miss Landon. I miss his smile, his scent, his warmth, and even the awkward way he danced at first. I thought I did the right thing and that after some months, the pain would go away, but I was wrong. I regret breaking things off. Would my misery really have been worse if I stayed with him long distance? Would my work as an intern have suffered? I'm not sure anymore.

When I chat online with Dominic or Val, it takes all my strength not to casually ask about the men's soccer team. My friends at KU know about my break-up of course, but they are kind enough not to pry. I have to avoid social media, but some nights I'm weak. When I peek at the story feeds, occasionally I'll see Steven with Ravi, and Landon pops up with them. Apparently, the team is doing very well this season.

I finish texting as Jung gets out of the bathroom. "Alright Dane, what are we doing tonight?" I look at him, confused. This guy is like a ball of energy, but he's coordinated when it's showtime. I don't have any friends in Manhattan, so Jung is one of the only people I talk to. Still, we rarely hang out after work.

"What do you mean?"

"Dane, we're in Philadelphia. Have you *been* to Philadelphia?"

"Uh, no. What's in this city?"

"I don't know…cream cheese? I've never been. Ooh! Let's go get cheesesteaks!"

I look at him dubiously. I'm not in the mood to go out, but frankly, I never am. These past four months, Jung and a few others have asked me to hang out, but each time I've come up with the lie that my aunt needs me. "I don't know."

"Come on, it's our last night here. I don't really wanna go out with anyone else. Please, please, please?" He dramatically holds his hands together and frowns at me. His pleading reminds me of someone I don't want to think about, but Landon was definitely more charming.

After a moment, I shrug. "I suppose I could eat."

"Yes!" he hisses, raising his fist slightly higher. I smile and get up to get dressed.

Jung and I walk three blocks down to an indoor food court that has rave reviews. Thirty minutes and two cheesesteaks later, we're sitting at a two-person table on the upper level eating dessert. I'm playing with the crumbs of my marshmallow rice cake while listening to Jung regale me with stories from his school.

"…and that's basically what competitive ballroom dance is." He takes a sip of water before returning to his large frozen yogurt with nuts and a cherry.

"Sounds intense," I reply.

"It can be." He pauses for a moment and looks around. No one is within ear shot, and I realize this setting is starting to feel a little too much like a date. "So. We've been working together for months, but I barely know Dane." I shrug. "Okay, let's start with the good stuff. Did you leave anyone special behind at college?"

Well, there it is. I'm not sure what to say. On the one hand, I broke up with Landon. On the other hand, I'm still not over him, and I definitely don't want to give Jung any false hope. He's cool, but I'm not interested in anyone right now.

I take a deep breath to speak, but I'm interrupted by Jung's chuckle. "So that's a yes."

I laugh as well. "Guilty."

"What's his name? Or we can use codenames like in middle school."

I giggle some more. "His name is Landon."

"Ooh, that's a good one."

"No, that's his real name. And we..." I roll my water bottle in my right hand. "We're not...It's complicated."

"Isn't it always?" Jung plays with the cherry stem in his hand. "Sorry, man, I swear I don't mean to be pushy. If you don't wanna talk about it that's fine. I just figured we might as well get to know each other better. If this pans out, we'll end up working at RDC next year."

"True." I relax my shoulders and stare at the remnants of my dessert. "It's not that. It's just been awhile since anyone's asked me about my boy troubles."

"I know that all too well. So what's troubling you about Landon?" I look up and notice he seems genuinely interested. Jung is a cool guy, and it's not like me telling him my problems will in any way make life worse for me.

"Well, let's start from the top..." For the next five minutes I tell him a truncated version of my relationship with Landon—the G-rated summary, anyway. I talk about how I was his TA, how he danced with me at a club, how I kissed him first, and how we started dating. Jung never interrupts me, and it's astounding how much drama I was holding in my heart that I hadn't let out.

"And that was the last thing he ever said to me." I exhale with a frown. "He got in the cab and I haven't spoken to him since."

"Ah," Jung replies, still eating. "Can I ask you a question that might make you think I'm an asshole?"

"Uh, sure?"

"Why'd you shoot yourself in the foot?"

My eyebrows furrow. "What do you mean? I broke up with him to focus on this internship."

"*EHH*," he buzzes, like we're on a game show and I failed. "That guy was willing to wait for you, so I'll need a better answer, bro." He continues to stare at his yogurt and scoop up more.

I look down at the table frowning. "He wasn't… He shouldn't have to wait around…"

"Shouldn't wait for you? Be with you? Why not? This guy is crazy about you."

"But he's not…" I play with some crumbs and stare at them intently, the truth getting caught in my throat. "He's a gorgeous athlete. Everyone loves him. I'm a half-blind dance major who's never been in a relationship. We were never meant to work out in the long term." I sniff and realize my eyes are getting wet.

"Dane, it's never gonna work until you *actually* 100 percent realize and accept that yes, this guy loves you." I look up to see him studying his yogurt. "Mmm, this is really good froyo. You should try some." He eats more, then stares

- The Moves We Make

at me, spoon still in his mouth.

What's Jung talking about? I accepted…Oh wait. I replay our entire relationship in my head. Not once did I ever let go of the fear he was too good for me. *I never actually accepted that Landon loved me. Shit.* It took me breaking up with him, four months of loneliness, and this guy with froyo in his mouth to make me realize it.

"Are you okay?"

"Oh fuck, Jung." I groan, rubbing my temple. "I never did accept his love. My fucking insecurities held me back."

"Don't we all have them," he mutters.

"Oh please," I retort, irritated. "You're fit and handsome with a symmetrical face. I'm the guy with only one functioning eye."

"Making me blush," he says, looking up and shrugging. "But seriously, don't talk about yourself like that. If you weren't good-looking I wouldn't have invited you out here on what was supposed to be a date."

My eyebrows jump. "Oh…"

"No, it's fine." Jung waves his hand in front of me in an attempt to dispel any weirdness. "I always suspected you were hung up on someone. Now that I know your story, it's clear that nothing romantic is happening here."

I wince. "Sorry."

"Don't apologize. Besides, every gay guy needs a fellow gay guy to be their platonic friend. That can be us!" I smile at him. "Now, let's talk plans. Operation *'Win back your man'* is underway." He grins and I giggle. Jung is a cool guy. I'm glad he's in my corner.

35: Landon

It's the day before Thanksgiving and I'm back home in Manhattan. I'm lying on my bed in just my boxers, hair probably a mess, playing on my Nintendo Switch. Going out with the guys three weeks ago was nice, and Sly put things in a new perspective, but I'm still mopey most days. While I want Dane to know I'm the real deal, I promised to leave him alone during his internship. That means I have to wait two more months before I can make any moves.

So here I am, lounging around the day before another boring holiday where my parents will no doubt bring family friends to meet my siblings. As I play a mind-numbing video game for the third hour in a row, I feel a sudden tug on my portable device; Link is hovering above me, yanking away my game.

"Hey, I was playing that!"

"Too bad."

I sit upright to see my brother towering next to my bed, the door open behind him. "Link, you have your own Switch."

"That's not why I'm here," he says, turning off my game and putting it down.

"Can you get out of my room and leave me alone please?" I whine, looking down.

"No." I look up at him and see an unimpressed face. "I left you alone all summer."

"Link, please I—"

"I left you alone when we went to the beaches and you acted like you were fine. I didn't call you out all those times Mom and Dad asked if you were okay and you lied. Landee, your fake smile is obvious as fuck, by the way."

"Link, what do you want?"

"I'm sick of you moping around. Come on. Let's go out, you and me."

"I'm kind of going through a rough time, a break-up."

"All the more reason to rebound!" He sits on the bed and slaps my knee with the back of his hand. "Let's go out to a bar and pick up girls."

"I broke up with Dane," I whisper, as if afraid someone nearby might find out I'm not straight.

"Then let's go to a gay bar!"

I stare at him skeptically. "You'd go with me to a gay bar?"

"Sure. I've been to plenty of gay bars." I'm filing away that piece of trivia for later. I can't process the idea of my younger brother also being queer, at least not right now.

I shake my head slightly. "Look, I just don't want to," I murmur and lie down on my side, clinging to my pillow. God, I wish Dane were here right now.

After a minute of silence I expect to feel the weight of my brother rising from the bed. Instead, I feel him still sitting there.

"Do you not want to hang out with me anymore?" Link's voice sounds so small right now it alarms me. I slowly get up to see him hunched over staring at the floor. "I know I'm not the best brother. I'm sorry Mom and Dad are always forcing me to talk to their friends. I should make more time to see you, even when you're in school." Shit, how long has he felt like this?

"Link, it's not you, seriously." He's still not looking at me, his shoulders still slumped. "You're a good brother, and I *do* wanna hang out with you."

"Really?" he mutters. He turns and looks right at me, his face filled with hurt. He's so tall and successful; sometimes I forget he's still my little brother. He's still the kid I taught how to spell 'Mississippi', how to make milk and cereal, and when it's okay to use the middle finger.

"Yeah! And in the spring I can visit you too. There's less soccer stuff happening then anyway."

"I've been reading about your team online. You guys might take it all the way this season."

"For real? You read about us?"

"Yeah. Meeting your boyfriend during our birthday party made me realize I don't pay attention to your life that much. None of us do." Damn, I didn't know how much I needed to hear that until now.

"Thanks, Link. But he wasn't my boyfriend back then."

"For real?" He turns toward me, eyebrows furrowed. "The way he looked at you at the party, I'd swear you two were already hooking up."

"No," I giggle. "We hadn't yet. But I think I already liked him at the time." I pull a piece of lint off my bed.

"Look, I'm down to hang out, but I don't think I'm ready to go to a bar or anything."

"Do you want to go do something else?"

An idea strikes me. It could be a disaster, but I don't think anything can make me feel worse.

"I think I know what I want to do," I smile. "Let's get dressed."

"I'm the one wearing pants here, not you." Link gets up, smirking, and walks out the door.

36: Dane

I walk into the men's dressing room still buzzing from the performance. The day before Thanksgiving is the first showing of *The Christmas Picturesque*, thus kicking off the most lucrative and busy season for the RDC Manhattan. While most nights I'm lonely and depressed, it's times like these I'm legitimately happy, where I know my place in the world. I want to be able to perform and teach the art of dance full-time here, in the arts capital of the East Coast.

I take off my shirt and wipe the sweat from my face as Jung sits down next to me. "Damn man, first show in the books. Can you believe we're actually living the dream? Being part of *The Christmas Picturesque*?!" He's taking off his clothes while I put on my pants.

"We're just understudies and stage-hands so far." I shrug.

"Yes, but we were *on* stage. And our names are on the roster! That's so dope!" I can't help but grin at the excitement bouncing off him. "Maybe one day this season, they'll let us take over the roles of the toy soldiers or the nutcracker army men!"

"Maybe." I take out my phone and aimlessly scroll through social media as a way to decompress after the big show. After one swipe, I see something that makes my heart stop for a moment.

I must be physically shaken because Jung asks, "What's wrong?" He leans in and looks down. On my phone is a social media story of Landon. He's right in front of this very theater, and it was uploaded three hours ago. He was here tonight at the show! He's posted a selfie of him with his brother, and the caption reads, *"The little bro and I managed to snag last minute tix to The Xmas Picturesque!"*

I stop breathing. There are a hundred thoughts buzzing in my head. Landon must have known I'd be here. My name is in the roster. He probably saw me on stage— being a stage-hand in the background, but still. For those few hours, Landon and I were under the same roof. Hell, he might even be right outside the building. Well, it's been a while since the show let out, so he's probably long gone.

"That's him? That's your boy?" Jung asks, snapping me back to reality. I nod vigorously, trying to catch my breath.

"What-wha...what should I do?" I stammer. I have to do something, right?

"Go call him! Call him right now!" Jung shakes my shoulders and leads me out to a nearby deserted hallway.

Hand shaking, I press dial on the one name I've been trying to avoid for so long. After two rings, I hear him pick up.

"Hello?" Landon sounds so confused, but I'd recognize his deep voice anywhere.

"Uh, hi... Landon?"

"Dane?! Are you okay? What's going on? Do you need help?" He sounds so worried. Of course, I break his heart, leave him for months, and the first thing he does when I call him is ask how he can help me. I was an idiot to ever break up with this man.

I shake my head. "No, no. I mean, I'm fine, I just uh...I wanted to chat."

"Oh...oh." He sounds calmer now, but confused.

"I saw on social media you were at the show tonight."

"Oh right. Um...about that. Link and I wanted to see it. We hadn't been in years. I'm sorry if that seemed intrusive." He sounds so apologetic it warms my heart. After hurting him, he's still looking out for me.

"No, it's not that! I'm glad you came. I wanted to see if you were still around."

"No, actually, we decided to take a cab back home. Did you need something?"

I hesitate for a moment. There's a million words in my heart because yes, I need something, and it begins and ends with the guy I can't stop thinking about. "Yeah. I need to talk to you. But I kind of wanted to do that in person."

"Sorry, we're um...We're almost home."

"Can I come visit? Just for a few minutes."

"Uhh..." He sounds reluctant, which is fair.

"I promise it will be short. I just need to tell you some things in person. I'll take a cab and then I'll go home. Please Landon." After a moment of silence, I press on. "Pretty please."

"Alright. If it's not gonna mess with your dance schedule or anything."

Yes! "It won't. I'm off tomorrow for Thanksgiving. I'll be at your place soon. Thank you Landon." I quickly shut off the phone, not waiting for him to change his mind.

My heart is thrumming with anticipation for this huge leap I'm about to take when I look up to see Jung. "Well?"

"I asked if I can see him in person now, tonight, at his place, and he agreed."

"Yes!" He pumps his fist in the air and smiles. "You have the letter?"

"On my phone."

"Alright! Get out of here and call a cab. Go. Shoo!" He pushes me down the hallway, and I chuckle. The last thing I hear before exiting down the stairs is Jung yelling, "Get your boy, Dane!"

I step out of the cab into the cold November darkness. I tried to take calming breaths the entire way, but my mind is still swarming with a dozen different scenarios of how this will play out—most of them heartbreaking. I'll understand if Landon tells me to fuck off, but something about our phone conversation gives me a fiber of hope. Is it possible he misses me too?

"Fuck, I hope so," I mutter as I ring the gate doorbell. The screen blinks and the gate unlocks, just as I see the house door open. The light inside reveals a silhouette and I stop breathing. I can't see his face, but I recognize the figure —that's my Landon.

As he approaches, I see he's wearing a hoodie and his hair is longer, but he's still the beautiful boy I fell in love with. Getting closer, I try to read his face. He looks confused and sad, but I can tell he's trying to mask it all.

"Landon," I whisper. "Uh, hi." I probably look like I've just run a marathon, but I can't help it. My heart is pounding rapidly because *he's here, oh my God, he's really here in front of me, oh my God!* My hand instinctively tries to reach for him, but I hold back.

"Dane." I snap out of it. Hearing him say my name, two feet in front of me but a million miles away, is equal parts restorative and agonizing. "You wanted to talk?" He sounds so defeated, like he failed a midterm.

I take a deep breath and pull out my phone. "Um yeah, I wrote down some stuff…Stuff I need to say." I open the app that has the letter Jung and I worked on. It lists all of the apologies and explanations I could think of, and hopefully it will be enough.

"Um, first and foremost," I begin, looking up at him. "I'm sorry." I study his face, but I can't read him, so I continue. "I'm an idiot. I regret ever saying goodbye to you." I try to read the rest, but the tears start to well up. The dam that blocked all my feelings for Landon is crumbling, and I can't do anything about it.

I sniff and wipe my eyes. "I could make up a million reasons about my internship and needing to be single to be professional, but that was all a lie. The truth is I never accepted that you loved me. But it took losing you to realize that yeah, you *did* love me. You made my life so much better at KU, and I want you to be by my side no matter where I am." I look up at him, but I can't see his face. My vision is getting blurry with tears.

"Landon, I love you. I'm sorry if I ever made you think I don't. I'm sorry I didn't say it before, but I do and…" My confession gets caught in my throat with a sob, and I shake my head. "I'm sorry for everything," I whisper.

I clench my eyes as hot tears fall down my face. There's so much I need to say but I just can't right now. Before I realize it, he's holding me in his arms and rubbing my back saying "Shh…" Having Landon hold me again feels like sunshine after a monsoon. It feels like being home.

After catching my breath on his shoulder and sniffing some more, I'm finally able to talk again. "I understand if you never want to speak to me again, or if I'm too late and you're dating someone else. But if you could find it in your heart to let me try again, I swear I'll never take you for granted. I'll accept any love or affection you have for me, for real this time." He pulls us apart slowly and gets a good look at me. I can't decipher his face as he pulls out his phone. Aw, shit.

I wipe my eyes. "Um, you don't have to show me pictures of your new girlfriend. I get it." I shrug, trying to sound casual. I deserve any pain he wants to throw at me, but this just seems out of character.

I hear Landon snicker—a good sign? "It's not pictures of a girl, Dane." He shows me his phone and I take a good look. It's a countdown app that shows a certain amount of days and hours left. I don't get it.

"I got this app when we broke up," Landon says. "It's counting the hours and days until you're back at KU. I was going to ask you out again." Landon is smiling, but I need him to clarify.

"What?"

"Dane, I told you I was going to wait for you and I meant it. I couldn't move on even if I tried. You have my heart, no take-backs." There's a buzzing in my ears that comes from shock and hope. Is Landon saying what I think he's saying?

Suddenly he looks up, and I tilt my head up as well. A small snow flurry has begun. "Well, look at that," Landon remarks. "Just like on our first date." He looks back down directly into my eye. "Do you remember?"

I beam at him and nod. "Yeah."

"So what do you say, Dana Poorweisz? Do you wanna start again? No messing around, just you and me? Together?" He takes my hand and laces his fingers with mine. A warmth courses through my body as I smile back at him.

I nod. "Yes, Landee Landon. I'm in love with you so...yes." He strokes my cheek gently, wiping away any remaining tears. Then, he pulls me in and kisses me, and my lips are exactly where they belong.

"Fuck...I've missed you so much," he mutters against my face in between kisses.

"Same. Oh God Landon...I'm so sorry." I pull apart and place my forehead on his. "I understand if you're mad or you hate me, but I swear I'll do everything to—"

"I don't hate you, Dane, I love you." He chuckles and kisses me again.

"I love you too. So damn much."

"I'll never get tired of hearing that," he quips, smiling against my mouth. We continue to kiss as the snow falls down and the pain in my heart starts to fade away.

"Hey! Love birds!" We break apart abruptly to see his brother yelling from the doorway. "Dinner's ready! Stop making out and come in here. It's freezing!"

We both laugh, and, holding hands, we walk inside.

37: Landon

That night we have a dinner of heated leftovers with Link, Kara, and Marta, because my parents are once again away. Tonight's meal is special, though, because Dane is by my side. *Oh my God, Dane is here with me, and he said he loves me and wants to start again, oh my God, yes!*

Going to see him at *The Christmas Picturesque* was not supposed to be some emotional manipulation. The truth is, I wanted to see him in his element, happy and on stage, with or without me. He only had a small role, but spying him in the back moving scenery around still made my heart skip a beat. Being in that audience made me realize that, yes, I'm still madly in love with him. I guess it's good I posted that selfie.

Now he's back, and all is right in the universe. My world is right here, wrapped in my arms, cuddled with me in my living room. Dane is leaning on my side on the big couch while Kara is sitting on the large chair and Link sits on a pillow on the floor. The TV is big enough, we're watching episodes of *Community*, and I'm happier than I've been in months. I constantly stroke his shoulder and he plays with the fingers in my other hand, reminding me of his presence; Dane is here with me now, and this isn't a dream. And oh yeah, we're in love.

After two episodes, the twins call it a night. They claim they're sleepy, but I'm pretty sure they're just giving us some privacy. I look down and see Dane checking his phone.

"You letting your aunt know you're staying the night?" In between episodes, I offered the guest bedroom to Dane. Since he had no work tomorrow, he could relax here for the night—sex or no sex, it was all good to me.

"Yup." He smiles at me. "I'm also texting Jung."

"Who?"

"He's my friend from RDC. My only friend really. He's actually the one who helped me sort out my feelings for you, and he's been *begging* me to call you so we could work it out. He's so cool. You'll like him."

"How much do *you* like him?" I don't appreciate the idea of some random, probably queer guy being all friendly with my Dane. "If you guys dated or hooked up, I won't hold it against you."

Dane smiles and strokes my face. "Babe, we're just friends. He may have been interested initially, but it was so obvious I was hung up on you that he didn't want to pursue it. More importantly..." He leans up and kisses me on the cheek. "I'm in love with you."

I smile and stare at him intently. My smile fades as I sit upright, getting a good look at him. The fear of losing him is creeping up again.

"What's wrong?"

I bite my lip, then whisper, "You're not gonna run away again, are you?"

"What?!" He sits upright, eyebrows furrowed in confusion.

"Nothing." I shake my head and smile. "Just forget it."

"Please tell me, Landee."

"It's just...I'm so happy you're back. But when I go back to KU, are you gonna...Like tomorrow, are you gonna decide this was a mistake? Are you going to break up with me again?" My eyes fill with tears. I hadn't realized how insecure I was until now.

"Baby, no," he whispers, holding my face with both hands. "I'm so, so sorry." He kisses my cheek and I feel myself get warmer. That's all it takes for Dane to make me feel safe again, like I'm finally home. "I love you, babe. You make me whole. I'm not letting you go again. Got it?"

He wipes away a tear from my cheek and I nod. I pull him in and hug him on the couch for another minute. I just need to hold Dane to know that this is real.

Dane spends the night in the guest bedroom without me sneaking in. We agreed that if this is going to work, we need to have boundaries. I can't just sneak in to sleep with him all the time, even if he's only a few feet away.

The next morning, after breakfast, Dane and I go on a short walk around the block, hand in hand. This neighborhood always felt so sterile, filled with jaded rich folks and tourists, but with my boyfriend back with me, it's not so bad. When we get home, my parents have finally returned, and several strangers are in the house setting up the Thanksgiving luncheon.

I spot my mom as she's directing some caterers on where to place the silverware. "Hey Mom."

"Hi honey. Oh!" Her gaze lands on Dane, and my

hand wrapped in his. "Well uh…Hello dear. You're…"

"Dane, ma'am," he replies.

"Right, Dane." Her eyes continue to dart between our faces and our held hands. "I assume you'll be joining us for Thanksgiving?"

Dane shrugs. "My aunt was cool with it. She's busy at her friend's house, so…yeah? If that's alright ma'am."

"Of course, honey. Any…*friend* of Landee's is welcome here." I smile and note her hesitation with the word friend. I'm sure they'll have questions, but that's a baby step for later. Today is all about Dane and me.

"Thanks, Mom."

"Of course. Now please, you boys go get dressed. The guests will be arriving in an hour. We have the pharmaceutical reps Mr. and Mrs. Ng, as well as the Scott-Griffiths and their daughter. Hopefully she'll hit it off with Link, or hell, even Kara. That reminds me, I should find out if Pauline and her wife are coming." She whips out her phone and trails off, leaving us.

We make our way upstairs to our respective rooms to get ready. I once again let Dane borrow an old suit of mine. We do have thirty minutes to kill all alone in my room, so, locking the door, I lure Dane into my bed, and he manages to give me something *else* to be thankful for this holiday.

After a delicious meal, we're in the living room playing a group game with my siblings. I'm holding a phone to my head and the others need to act out what animal is on the phone, while my job is to guess what word is on display. We're in hysterics after one round where they all had to act like crabs and I hand the phone to Link. It's genuinely a good time, and I haven't played a game with my siblings in over a year.

Before we can start a new round, however, my mom walks in. "Link, honey, the Ng family wants to talk to you about your latest modeling contract!" She waves and hollers and I look to see my brother's face drop.

"Uh, Mom!" I spin around. "Can this please, please wait? Link was about to go and we're in the middle of this. I swear we'll be done soon." Everyone seems taken aback by this. I can't remember the last time someone told my mom to wait before introducing one of the twins.

After a moment of confusion, my mom simply nods and says, "You kids come outside when you're ready." She leaves and I turn to see my brother, pleasantly surprised.

"Alright, your turn, bro," I announce, sitting back on the couch next to Dane. Link smiles and presses a button on the phone, and soon, the rest of us are laughing, hopping up-and-down like kangaroos.

That night, I'm waiting on the curb with Dane for his ride-share. I offered to drive him or to pay, but he insisted on doing it himself. This is part of our agreement; we both need to find a way to define our relationship, all while being professional and independent when we're apart. The snow on the ground has melted, but it's still cold. I wrap my arm around Dane while I lean against the gate.

"Our first holiday in the books."

"Hopefully the first of many. You sure your parents are gonna be cool with you being...you know...with a guy?"

"They'll deal. Besides, you heard my mom. She

was down for Kara to hook up with one of their friend's daughters." We both chuckle. "Kara is straight, I think. Link, not so sure."

"You guys all seem to be getting along." I look over to see him already smiling. "Things okay at home?"

I shrug. "Yeah. And now that I'm no longer mopey because *someone* finally admitted they love me—" I tickle his side for good measure and he giggles—"home life can keep getting better."

I wait a second, then lean in and kiss him gently. Just like that cold February night, kissing him tastes so sweet. I never felt genuine at school and I never felt seen at home, but with Dane in my life, I've found the courage to be an authentic version of myself, at school and with my family. I pull back as I'm overcome with all this emotion. How does this guy, someone I've known for less than a year, continue to take my breath away?

Dane wipes a tear from my face. "What's wrong, babe?"

"Nothing's wrong. You're beautiful, and I have you back. How can I ask for anything more?"

"Landee, I hope one day to be worthy of everything you've given to me."

"You are, Dane. I love you so much. Please believe that."

He solemnly nods. "I believe it. I accept your love, and I love you too."

Just then, the ride-share pulls up. I give Dane a quick kiss and a big hug and let him go. Unlike last time, this doesn't feel like the end. It's our newest beginning.

Epilogue: Dane

The summer sun shines over the inner courtyard of the Landon house and the latest pop music plays over the speakers. I walk over to the food and drink table to see Jung awkwardly standing there, holding a cup.

"Hey man!" I greet him cheerfully as I grab a plastic cup and start pouring myself a drink. "You enjoying yourself?"

"Yeah. I mean, well, I would more if I knew anyone here." Jung shrugs and takes another sip.

About seven months have passed since the Thanksgiving eve where I showed up here to beg Landon for forgiveness. He doesn't like when I word it that way, he claims it was a cute declaration of feelings. Getting back to KU was equal parts cold, aggravating, and satisfying. I had gotten used to living in New York City despite making a grand total of one good friend at RDC, and I loved dancing on a professional level. Still, that means nothing compared to being back on campus with my friends and my boyfriend.

Landee Landon is very much my boyfriend, and we're very much in love.

After Thanksgiving, the month and a half where he was at KU and I was back in Manhattan wasn't actually that bad. We missed each other, but we texted and phone chatted a lot. I made sure to keep him up-to-date with my life, and he did the same. In fact, the KU men's soccer team were regional champions this year, which is a big deal apparently. I'm so proud of my boyfriend and the rest of his teammates, most of whom have become my friends as well.

Being back at school with Landon waiting for me really was fantastic. I got a single dorm again and was able to finish the few credits I needed to graduate with the rest of our friends. My parents teared up at the ceremony, taking pictures nonstop of all of us in our gowns. Speaking of, my mom and dad have been getting along great with Landee since I officially introduced him as my boyfriend. They're content to know I have someone who makes me happy. Meanwhile in Manhattan, Landon's family has been so warm and welcoming to me whenever I'm around. His parents don't think it's weird Landee is bisexual now, and his relationship with his siblings is stronger than ever. My boyfriend claims it's because I gave him the confidence to be compassionate and understanding, but I know he did it all on his own.

Graduating from college was an amazing achievement, and so was snagging a full-time RDC position. I start in a week, and Jung and I are happy to not be the new kids anymore. We may even get proper roles at *The Christmas Picturesque* this year! I'm still officially staying with my aunt until I can find my own apartment, but I spend half of my nights right here at the Landon house.

That's where we are today for the huge graduation celebration Landee's parents have thrown us.

There's catering, balloons, a selfie-station, some board games, and plenty of Korham-University-themed decorations—Mrs. Landon doesn't do a half-baked party. I'm honored to be a guest, but I'm more proud of Landee for inviting all of his friends into his home. I look around and spot Kareem and his girlfriend playing a party game with Link and Kara. Across from them, I see Dominic chatting with Omar and Ravi.

"So who's that?" Jung points to someone across the courtyard discreetly. Apparently we're people-watching now.

"That's Jonathan, Tisha's boyfriend."

"And that guy with the kid?"

"That's Wei. He's a music professor at KU, but he's really chill. When we found out he was coming down for vacation, we invited him, his sister, and his nephew to swing by. The guy next to him is his boyfriend."

"Aww, they look happy." Just then, Ravi and Omar rush past us, presumably to the front door. "Who are those guys? Soccer boys?"

"Yup. Both taken."

Dominic strolls up to us with a frown on his face. "I was talking to them! And then they got a text saying the O'Rourke brothers have finally arrived, and all of a sudden I'm invisible!"

I laugh and put my arm around Dominic. "Aww, can you really blame young hearts, Dominic?"

"I swear, one day I'll find my own bisexual college jock."

"Maybe you'll have your chance in grad school!"

"A boy can only hope." Dominic looks up and fans himself while I chuckle at him.

"By the way, this is my friend Jung. Jung, meet

Dominic."

Jung shakes his hand. "Nice to meet you."

"Likewise." Dominic picks up a cup. "So did Dane force you to attend this big old couples' fest as well?"

"It's not a couples' fest!" I protest, rolling my eyes. "In fact, Jung here is single." I put my hand on his shoulder and Jung makes a guilty face.

My eyebrows shoot up. Before I can ask, I hear the sound of someone clapping in the corner. We all turn to my boyfriend waving his hand near the sound system.

"Attention! Attention, everyone!" The music dies, and everyone turns to look at him. "I have a few words I want to say. First of all, thank you to everyone who showed up. Thank you to my parents for hosting this event. It's been a wild ride at KU these past four years. College is the time to define yourself and really explore your interests. As most of you are aware, I discovered a *lot* about myself in the past couple of years."

There's a smattering of laughter, but I don't bother to look around, I only have eyes for Landee. In the sunlight, he's just as gorgeous as ever. He clears his throat and continues. "I just want to say, I hope the friends I made at KU on the soccer team and at various classes stick by me. To my soccer friends, you're my brothers in arms, and nothing will change that. Cheers!" He raises a cup, and everyone else follows suit, with echoes of "*Cheers!*" heard all around.

"Lastly, I want to thank one person in particular. I never felt comfortable in my own skin at home or at school. Then I met someone truly amazing." My skin starts to prickle as he looks directly at me. I can't help but smile back at him.

"I met a guy who was patient with me, even when I was learning to dance; a guy who played video games with me when I was too nervous to open up. He challenged me to be a better person but continues to support me every day. Because of you, I'm not that loud-mouth anymore who always pushed people away. At least, most days I'm not." The room murmurs with laughter, and nearly everyone has turned to look at me. "Dane, with you, I'm the best version of myself. No matter where life takes us, just know that I'm a better man because of you. I love you, Dane. Thanks for loving me too."

There are *"aww"*s and applause as Landee steps closer. I meet him halfway and kiss him briefly before I hug him tightly. At some point, someone puts on a slow song and Landon breaks apart from me.

"Wanna dance with this soccer boy?"

"Well there are a few things I need to teach you still." I look up and tap my chin.

"Like slow dancing?" Landon chuckles as he puts his hands on my waist.

"Now you're catching on," I reply with a grin, putting both hands on his shoulders. As we sway, Ravi and Steven, Tisha and Jonathan, and several other couples join us in the middle of the courtyard.

As we dance, I recall not too long ago feeling hollow, like I could never be worthy of love. Ever since Landee Landon came into my life, all of that changed. With him by my side, I can't wait for all the adventures we're going to have, whether it's in New York City, visiting KU, or anywhere else.

"You're not a bad dancer, Landee." I smirk, looking into his eyes.

"Well, I learned from the best." We smile into a kiss. "I love you, Dane. You've driven me crazy since the moment we met, and I wouldn't change a thing."

Blushing, I remember the words I've learned to recite to him over the past six months. "I accept that you love me, and I hope you accept that I love you too."

"Glad to hear it. I'd like to hear it tomorrow, the day after, and decades from now."

I kiss him again. "I think that can be arranged, babe."

The End

Thank You

Dear Reader,

Thank you so much for going on this journey with me! Once again, this has been a labor of love, and I'm ecstatic to finally have Landon and Dane's journey out there for the world to see!

Check the next two pages for links to all my socials so you can get plenty of insight about the "Artists and Athletes" universe and whatever other works I have brewing. I love talking to people about my books and I tease and spoil *constantly*. Read on for some links to my other works as well. Book 3 promises to be a little bit different—I think the *students* at Korham University aren't the only ones who deserve to find love, don't you agree?

Never stop loving life and never stop reading,
    CD Rachels

* * *

— — —

Acknowledgments

Rachel and Rod, thank you, I wouldn't be here without your encouragement. Catherine and Karen, thanks, you took my writing to the next level. Molly, thanks for chatting with me at odd hours. Ivy, thanks for helping me with GoodReads. Natalie, thanks for being my main girl since we fumbled through advanced ballet together. All of you Chill Discoursians, your support means the world to me.

Other Works

Other Works by CD Rachels

Want to know what happened last semester with Ravi and Steven?

Read "The Lines We Draw" (Artists and Athletes book 1) to find out more.

Want the next installment of the series? I bet you want to know all about our favorite Athletics Center facilities manager...

Check out "The Strings We Play" (Artists and Athletes book 3) for more.

About the Author

About the Author

CD Rachels has been coming up with stories since he was little. At first it was all about superheroes and pocket monsters, but his genre of choice has expanded since puberty.

He's been consuming young adult gay fiction since he was a teen, but within the past five years, he's moved up to the big leagues of gay adult romance. In 2020 during quarantine, he burned through more male/male romance books than he ever had in the previous 29 years combined.

He lives in New York City with the love of his life and works in health insurance. When he's not reading and writing, he's playing board games and practicing music. He is honored to become a published author, and if you're reading this, your support means so much to him that his skin is buzzing, but in a good way!

Want to see all of the promos for future works?

Follow him on Instagram: @cdrachels

Want to chat with him and get ALL of the spoilers?

Follow his Facebook fan group: CD Rachels' Chill Discourse Room

Drop a review on Goodreads!

Follow his Goodreads profile here

A review on Bookbub would be sweet too!

Follow his Bookbub profile here

CPSIA information can be obtained
at www.ICGtesting.com
Printed in the USA
LVHW052058070722
722996LV00004B/393